The Devil

Is A

Liar

Author: Mistry Troutman

ISBN: 978-1-387-04740-0

This book was printed in the United States of America.

Table of Contents

Prologue 4
The Devil Is A Liar 4
CHAPTER 1 6
CHAPTER 2 13
CHAPTER 3 24
CHAPTER 4 38
CHAPTER 5 51
CHAPTER 6 60
CHAPTER 7 66
CHAPTER 8 79
CHAPTER 9 91
CHAPTER 10 102
CHAPTER 11 109
CHAPTER 12 116
Falling Up 126
Epilogue 127

DEDICATION

This book is dedicated to my parents, Christine and the late Lee "Bubba" Robertson. You have always been examples and demonstrations of what love, commitment, and sacrifice truly look like. I am so thankful that God chose you to be my Mama and Daddy. I love you so much.

ACKNOWLEDGEMENTS

First of all, I thank God in all of His splendor and glory. You made it all possible.

Deep love and appreciation goes to my four sons. Kevin, Derrick, Devery, and Marcus; all I see are Gods chosen men of valor and honor. To my grandchildren, my heartbeats, Grandma loves all 10 of you. I pray God's best for you and know that you are all precious to me.

To the World's Greatest Brother, Christopher, you have always been my hero. I love you.

I would also like to thank my childhood friends and family members who have made many incredible imprints in my heart. Mentioning your names in this book was just a small tribute. I am so grateful for our "coming up", the good old days.

Patricia D. Wilkins, Carol Russell, and Bettye Williams; thank you for drowning out the lies of the enemy. Your covenant relationship; personal and ministerial, from the beginning, added value to my life. No words could ever express what you mean to me, and the life lessons I've learned from our connection.

Restoration of Hope-Next Level Ministries, the best church this side of heaven, thank you.

I would like to thank Diangela Byrd who initially helped me organize some thoughts. Teresa Jordan; you read and edited rough drafts, listened to my ideas, encouraged my dreams, and supported every effort to bring it to pass, thank you.

To the late Ann Jones, you told me what God said about me at an early age. Thank you for encouraging me to be the best me. My memory of your love for Jesus, and your relationship with the Holy Spirit continue to inspire me today.

To my spiritual mother, Evelyn Fain, I love you, and I appreciate you to the utmost. Thank you for covering me in prayer.

To my spiritual sons and daughters, prayer warriors, and intercessors, I love you. Thank you for loving the God in me.

Tashi Robinson, thank you for all that you do. You captured the vision.

Prologue

The Devil Is A Liar

I don't know when it happened, I just know it did. At that moment breathing became almost impossible. As the room got smaller, all the weight from my shoulders shifted to my chest. I felt my neck and chest getting wetter as the tears flowed continuously and unchecked. The burning in my chest increased. I prayed for the heart attack to come and take me out instead. That way, I wouldn't have to explain. That way, my family wouldn't have to lie about it later and say that I had been diagnosed with cancer. That way, escape from shame and humiliation would be a certainty. But after a while the burning stopped and was replaced by sharp stabbing pains.

I could still see, even though it was nearly impossible. So, to keep from stumbling into something or someone, I just silently slid to the floor, nearly collapsing as I re-played the words repeatedly. What was I going to do now? Who was going to help me? How could this be happening to me? What would I say to my Big Mama? Who was going to take care of my babies? As I lay numbly on the floor, I heard someone crying; no sobbing, and it sounded like a wounded animal in a trap. I tried to say something to God and I realized the sounds were coming from me. Couldn't talk and sob at the same time. Help me somebody, please, please help me. I don't want to die. I forgot to tell my babies that I loved them.

I don't know the last time I hugged Lil Bruh. Did I kiss Big Mama on the cheek last week? I've been so busy at work that I didn't return my girlfriends' calls. I will never get to talk to Oprah. I will not sing with CeCe. President Carter had not read my memo on "How to Save the World". So, what was I going to do? How much time did I have left? I cannot believe this! Why me? I have been through so much trouble and pain in my life. This is not fair! But why should I expect anything differently? I came into this world befriended by affliction and adversity. I guess that's the same way that I'm heading out.

CHAPTER 1

Psalm 127:3
Behold, children are a heritage from the LORD,
the fruit of the womb a reward.

I am ugly. I've always been ugly. Big Mama said that's why my birth Mama didn't want me. I was found down by the old arch bridge on the south side of the track. I don't know where I come from or who I came from. When I was about eight months old Big Mama and Lil Bruh rescued me at the water's edge. While they were on a fishing trip, Lil Bruh saw me punching my fists in the air. He says I was fighting my way out of the blankets someone had wrapped me in. Funny now thinking about it; that was probably the only time I ever tried to fight for myself. They brought me back to their house.

The people who left me there were probably waiting the first eight months of my life to see if I would grow into some cuteness; but I never did. So being ugly was my lot in life. I was okay with everything that went along with being ugly because I believed that's all I could ever be. I mean that's what the devil said. Every since I was knee high to a junebug he couldn't wait to tell me about myself. "You will never be anybody, you're ugly! You will never have anything, you're ugly! You just ain't no good, you're ugly! You are stupid, dumb, and ugly! Nobody loves you, you're ugly! You are better off dead and they should have left you at the water's edge!"

These statements were the beginning lines on the pages of every chapter in my life. It would take me a long time to stop reading that book, close it up, and tell the author, "Devil, you are a liar!" In my own way, and in my own time, I want to tell you a little bit about me and some of the people in my life. It's not a pretty story, but it is what it is.

We lived in Red Ash, Georgia. There was nothing particularly special about it; a small town right off the main highway going to Atlanta. The railroad track was in the center of town. As a young girl, this always puzzled me. Who builds a town around a railroad track? Or was the town here first? There wasn't a social or ethnic dividing line. Blacks and whites lived near the highway, while blacks and whites lived near the railroad tracks.

The most noticeable structure near the railroad tracks was the white two-story building next to the wash house. The black people's church, (not even the good Lord could get the people together much back then), owned it. It was intended to provide rooms for visiting preachers initially. But years ago, when the preacher ran off with the church secretary and the church money, the trustees and deacons decided to let anyone who had some dollar bills be able to get a room there. The few black families that lived in Red Ash were predominantly railroad men and loggers. The majority of white Red Ash citizens were mostly retired people from up North.

The white folks were nice enough for the most part; but many times, the older ones made you feel as if you were visiting and had worn out your welcome. They weren't friendly, but they were not openly mean either…. except Mr. Robert. He was nasty and mean. Nasty because he was known to spit on black people and mean because he seemed to get such joy out of it. He owned the small-town grocery store where most of his customers were old black people. Big Mama said the only reason she went in his store was because he had the freshest meat and the prettiest greens. Yes, I know, don't say it. I was thinking the same thing too. So, I get to pay you to disrespect me. Seems like a mighty high price to pay for some neck bones and collards.

The house we lived in resembled a big yellow square box. I used to call it the sunshine house; since even in the wintertime it was sunny. It seemed like a huge spotlight was always shining on it. There was a big front porch with a swing on one end and a long metal flower pot on the entire width of the opposite side. Several wooden rocking chairs were lined along the wall. Lil Bruh was always pulling them toward the edge of the porch so the back of the chairs would not hit against the wall. Big Mama did not allow that. She would holler from the inside of the house and run outside to pop us with her dish rag if we got too excited while rocking. I would sit for hours counting and rocking back and forth. Each day I would rock until I lost the count. I did this everyday until the back of my thighs would itch and have little ridges on them. I loved rocking in those chairs. I loved numbers too. I loved counting. Lil Bruh said I had a head for numbers.

The house was built high off the ground and it had 12 steps leading to the front door. Because the house was built high off the ground, I would often crawl underneath and sit for hours in my imaginary world. I was a dreamer, a make-believer. I could imagine things, people, sounds, and scents so vividly. My imaginary friends were not imaginary. Of course, I didn't tell anybody that for a long time. Big Mama always said that I was different. But I would talk with them and in my mind, they would show me pictures or movies about people and things. If I paid attention, I would see it again, at least it would happen for real. Some of the pictures were pretty, and some of them were scary.

Big Mama and Lil Bruh real names are Charlie Mae and Charlie McIntyre. They have been married for a long time. They have 2 sons, Ira and J.C. McIntyre. They live a long, long way from us because we hardly ever see them. It's only 3 times that they visit. That's Mother's Day, Thanksgiving, and the Day of Trouble. Whenever something goes wrong, they show up. Big Mama and Lil Bruh having trouble is a rare thing. Everybody gets along with them. One time the guys came when the shed was broken into. One time they visited when somebody stole Lil Bruh's railroad check out of the mailbox. One thing about them, maybe two things; you never see them come or go and they never stay for long. They are nice enough to me, but they are nothing like Lil Bruh and Big Mama. Some folks around here say that J.C. and Ira are in the mob. I don't know about that, but they look like they mean business.

I loved Big Mama. She was pretty, funny, and soft. She always smelled like peppermint. Her voice was deep and warm. They didn't call her Big Mama because of her stature, but because of her heart. Everybody loves Big Mama, because Big Mama loves everybody. She will take in folk off the street, bring them in, feed them and give them clothes too. She says that's her ministry. Something else about her is that she loves to sing. When she sings, and that was pretty much all the time, as you listened it didn't matter what was going on in your life, you would end up feeling better.

Your eyes would automatically close to take in the notes, the beats, and the moans. She loved Jesus and she would let you know it. Many times, when she was alone in the kitchen she would be talking to somebody. When asked, she would say she was just talking to the Master. I never saw Him, but she did. I know that she was talking to somebody! Her face would light up and sweat would break out on her skin; because she would get excited when she spoke about Him. I didn't know much about Him, but I liked hearing her talk to Him. Sometimes late at night I would hear her sitting on the porch mumbling to Him.

I couldn't hear what He was saying, but it must have been funny because she laughed a lot. Not only would she sing to Him, but she would talk to Him too. She would call Him up and ask Him to be her Friend. Often, I would hear her ask Him to hold her hand. Since I didn't see Him I assumed that Big Mama had an imaginary Friend too. All I know, I loved to hear her sing. She didn't mind it either. In the morning, at night, in the kitchen, on the porch, to Lil Bruh, to me and anyone else, she would sing. But she did not sing to anyone like she sang to Him.

As much as Big Mama loved to sing, I believe Lil Bruh loved to make people laugh. He could tell some jokes and crazy stories. He was my hero. As a little girl, I assumed that the sun showed up in the morning because Lil Bruh told it to. He was the next best thing to sliced bread and strawberry ice cream. He would have me laughing so hard until my face hurt. On purpose, I would try not to laugh and just hold it in, and then he would tickle me. Many times, I had to run to get away from him to keep from peeing on myself. Lil Bruh could not catch me either since he only had one real leg. The other one was made of wood. He told me that the anteater had bitten his leg off because he was too sweet; sweet as sugar. Of course, I believed him. Since everybody knows ants liked sugar I knew it had to be true. Besides, many times Big Mama would not let him eat certain foods during supper. She would say, "Lil Bruh, you know you got that sugar. Put that sweet bread down". He would just laugh and make a joke. Like I'm telling you, he was always making jokes and laughing. I asked him one day why he always laughed. He said it kept him from crying. It worked because I had never seen him cry.

Now Red Ash had some interesting people, Miss Carolyn being one. She and Big Mama met while working at the church boarding house. Big Mama cooked, and Miss Carolyn cleaned up. Miss Carolyn lived across the street from us. She and Big Mama were best friends. They would watch the stories together. I say together, but not really together. They would come out on the front porch of their home and holler at each other when the commercials came on. They would continue discussing what had just happened and complaining to each other about how silly the people were. I never understood why they didn't just sit at each other's house. It made more sense to me. Everyday at the same time, you could hear them fussing about the crooks, the skanks, and the idiots. Everyday Big Mama would say she's not fooling with them crazy folk.

Everyday Miss Carolyn would nod her head and say she wasn't either. It got bad especially on Fridays. But it never changed. They met up on the front porch the following Monday as if they had never mentioned not watching it again. On Sunday night before the television went off, Lil Bruh called it the short place, they would be waiting to see if somebody got shot or if the one in a coma would wake up. Sure enough, the next day, Miss Carolyn would holler over to Big Mama's that it was time. Nobody would bother them for those hours. I liked Miss Carolyn. She was always nice to me. She would give me peanut butter cookies and chewing gum. She always told me to be a good little girl. I knew she kept reminding me to be good because I was ugly, and one thing about it, ugly girls had to be nice. It didn't matter. Always polite, because that's how Big Mama raised me, I would tell her thank you and take my treats to my cigar box in the shed.

The shed was at the back of the house. It was my favorite place other than my sand castle under the house. I liked to spread my cookies on the table to tell a story. They were big yellow cookies with a man on a horse. Penny wheels are what they were called. Sometimes the man would be riding a horse. Sometimes he was standing by it. He wore a hat, and then again there were cookies in which he held a hat in his hand. I imagined that he was riding to get me. I don't know why I wanted him to come get me. Probably because I had heard Big Mama tell Miss Carolyn that she could forget about a man coming on a horse to get her. Miss Carolyn always laughed and shook her head. My imaginary friend would shake her head at me too.

You could find everything in the shed. Big Mama had towels, curtains, pillows, clothes, shoes, and pots stacked on one side. She said you never knew when somebody might need things. There were tables, chairs, a bed, some books, a medicine cabinet and boxes of magazines. On the walls were hundreds of pictures, menus from favorite restaurants, receipts from places they had went to in Atlanta, and ticket stubs from the picture show. My favorite picture was the one I had drawn with the big red barn, the orange butterflies, and the white flowers. The colors seemed to float off the picture and stand in front of me. I could trace the outlines of the picture in my mind for hours. Every chance I got I told Lil Bruh that one day I was going to find that barn.

He laughed and told me to eat my cookies and go play somewhere. But he would have a strange look on his face when he said it. Lil Bruh had been all over the world, but I believe one of his favorite places was the shed too. He had an old recliner placed in front of an ice chest. He hid his honey buns, RC cola, peanuts, and Mr. Longboys from Big Mama in there. He would sit and nod in that raggedy chair for hours. I sat, colored, and ate my penny wheel cookies. He did not tell Big Mama about my cigar box and I did not mention his ice chest. All was right with the world. We didn't know that trouble was about to hit our house. Life as we knew it would never be the same.

CHAPTER 2

Psalm 46: 1-5

God is our refuge and strength, a very present help in trouble. Therefore, we will not fear though the earth gives way, though the mountains be moved into the heart of the sea, though its waters roar and foam, though the mountains tremble at its swelling. Selah - There is a river whose streams make glad the city of God, the holy habitation of the Most High. God is in the midst of her; she shall not be moved; God will help her when morning dawns.

That day that Ira and J.C. McIntyre came to visit would be the same day that I started hating green frogs and ginger ale. I'll never forget that day. It was the first time I saw Lil Bruh cry. It wasn't Mother's Day. It wasn't Thanksgiving. I got lost that Monday morning. I was about 4 years old and I was on my way to the fish creek with Lil Bruh. Big Mama was home waiting on her stories to come on. They had seen in the short place that somebody was going to get shot. She was not about to miss that. Sometimes I thought that Bill and Bertha Bauer in good old Springfield meant more to her than me. On the other hand, she also stayed home because she was tired. She said they had got the butter from the duck today at the boarding house. She was so tired that she was sitting on the settee with her bra still on. The first thing Big Mama did on the days she had to work was take her bra and shoes off as soon as the screen door hit the hook. She said the church was having a special meeting and everybody and their grandmother was there. So, the preacher had asked her to cook extra.

Lil Bruh always made things an adventure, something fun, and I was always ready to join in. I kissed Big Mama and Lil Bruh pulled one of her plaits and we headed to the fish creek. Lil Bruh grabbed our equipment and we started on our way. He made up a counting game and I had such an enjoyable time with him. He was amazed that I could count so well. Even then I wanted to please him, and I concentrated on those numbers to prove that I was smart, good, and worthy. Looking back now I

realize that my desire to be loved and approved began at such an early age.
Sidebar: Mothers, Dads, Grandparents, Aunties, Uncles, and others; if you notice a child in your care or the care of others, who constantly looks for attention and validation, check them out. It means something.

Okay, back to the story.

I counted the number of steps we took while walking towards various points of interest. We stopped at Mr. Robert's store to get our lunch as we were on our way to catch our supper. I was standing by the back door while Lil Bruh went to buy our ginger ale, soda crackers, hook cheese, honey bun, and vienna sausages. That was some good eating, and I loved me some ginger ale! He told me to count and tell him how long it took him to get back. We didn't go in the front door of the store because old man Robert didn't really like it. He had a little stool out front where he chewed tobacco and "accidently" spit when certain people walked in to buy stuff. So, Lil Bruh would always take me to the back because he said he didn't want Ira and J.C. to skin nobody. He told me to stay right where I was, and I would have if I had not forgotten what number I was on before I saw the frog.

I was determined to catch the tiny green frog that jumped over my foot. I had never seen that color green before. It was vibrant, pretty and shiny. It glowed against the dark red clay dirt that was packed along the side of the back stoop. I wasn't afraid of it because I helped Lil Bruh dig up worms whenever we went fishing all the time. Running behind the frog I was not paying attention to where I was going. Wherever the frog hopped, I ran. It was as if the frog waited for me to catch up with it, beckoning for me to follow it.

Every time I would almost cup it in my hands, it danced in the air out of my reach. Before I knew it, I was standing next to some empty boxes and crates in the alley behind Mr. Robert's store. Man, I almost had it. Taking a minute to try and figure out where it went, all of a sudden, my legs were pulled out from under me. My head hit the ground so hard that I couldn't see anything; no stars, no moon, no sun. Blank, no color, not even that black background behind my eyelids. The ground was cold and wet on my back. I could taste my tongue. Each of my senses was arguing with the other one. Such conflict. Not only could I not see but I could not hear either. It was as if I could FEEL the sounds and, TOUCH what I was hearing. Reaching out to touch the noises, I tried to hold it inside my head but it would not stay. It leaped out of my mouth silently. At that same moment, I felt a weight; something heavy across my chest, and all the way down to cover my thighs. I could not move. I could not breathe. I could not speak. I could not hear.

How long can I hold my breath? I figured it out too late that I wasn't holding my breath. It was. The weight on my chest confused me because the numbers didn't come out right. I squeezed my eyes, tears appeared, and the disagreements ceased between my senses. I opened my eyes again. I saw the green frog staring at me. It laughed. Instantly it disappeared. In the next second IT happened. I LOST ME! At that moment, young little Imogene Marie Jones was gone. She was wrenched away from me. When the ripping started, Mr. Pain took me somewhere else. When did my imaginary friends get here? Suddenly another Hand hid me from Mr. Pain. I had escaped and Imogene was gone too. I was waving goodbye to Mr. Pain when The Hand pulled me into the water. The water was purple. It was so pretty. I did not see where Imogene went. But I knew that she was safe. I'll have to look for her later.

I had to keep up with my imaginary friend who was not imaginary. At first the purple water was cold. I got used to it because I went to sleep tucked inside the Hand. Before closing my eyes, I saw Imogene. She was crying and reaching for me. As the purple water warmed around me, I grasped Imogene's fingers and placed them in the Hand. It took her away and kept her in that quiet place for a long time. In the quiet place Mr. Pain was not able to get to me either. The Hand poured purple water over me and I tried to count how long it took me to fall asleep in the quiet place. Right before I woke up, I saw Imogene crouching behind a big rock. I knew that she was calling out to me, but I couldn't hear what she was saying. It would take me the next 20 plus years to find that out. But that's another story.

In the meantime, I smelled dirt. I tasted dirt. Dirt was all over me. Dirt was in my eyes. Dirt was in my mouth. I had dirty eyes. I had a dirty mouth. I was dirty. I still could not see, but I could hear. Lil Bruh was here in the dirt with me, and he was crying. I heard me crying too. As he turned me over, his tears dropped on my face and mixed with my dirt. What happened to the little green frog? Why was Lil Bruh crying? He never cried.
I remember him carrying me from the alley. His chest was singing a song of beats; like the sound the drums at church made. Let me tell you, I know that he carried me because I could not walk. My legs were wet and sticky. I smelled like old dishwater. Not only did I smell like old dishwater but my "pocketbook" was hurting. That's what Big Mama called it. She said my pocketbook held something priceless and I had to always take care of it. Somehow even then I knew that I had lost something valuable. Not only did I know that, but I also knew that I hated little green frogs. If that frog had never hopped over my big toe, my pocketbook would still be priceless.

I woke up to Big Mama screaming and yelling. So much has happened, and much time has past, but I can't even tell you how we got home. I remember Big Mama grabbed me from Lil Bruh and ran to the back porch. I can still see his face. He was crying. Big Mama was praying now because I heard her say His name. In the big tin tub, she poured water and her healing salt. I heard her singing and crying at the same time. Lil Bruh stayed in the kitchen. Miss Carolyn came running from around the house and her hands were shaking so bad. The curtains were open and from the back porch I could see Lil Bruh standing at the sink. He was slumped over and I knew he needed Big Mama's Friend to hold him too. I don't know how I knew that at 4 years old, but I did. Big Mama had often said that there was something different about me anyway. She said I had been here before. She was always talking like that. But I knew that Big Mama was holding us all together with her song. She was asking the Precious One not to leave us alone. She spread the healing salt all over my skin.

Everywhere her hands touched left a trail of fire and a cool breeze at the same time. Big Mama sent Miss Carolyn away to run and find Miss Flossie. Big Mama said too much life was flowing from me and HE had told her to send for her. She was the local medicine woman and midwife. She could find more remedies in her front yard than you could get from the drug store man. It was rumored that doctors sent folk to her late at night when they were ailing from certain illnesses. Everybody in Red Ash knew she was one smart woman. Big Mama said she was born too soon. She said because Miss Flossie was a woman there were things she couldn't do, and places she couldn't go. She saved a lot of lives though. But that's another story.

After some time, Big Mama gathered me from the tin tub on the back porch and folded me into a great big towel. She was still crying. She was still talking to Him because I heard His name rush past her lips. I did not say a word. I couldn't. When Big Mama says His name, I just listen. She told me that He was my Friend and insisted that He could do anything, and that He loved me. But I didn't talk to Him, didn't know him like that. When we went into the house, she stopped in the kitchen and put her healing salt on Lil Bruh hands too. He was still crying. Before any of this had happened, I didn't recognize what agony and suffering looked like. But I was being introduced to the two of them in a big way. Big Mama said that I would be okay. I didn't know who she was trying to convince or who she was speaking to, and looking at Lil Bruh's face, I think he was wondering who she was talking with also. He took me from her, and carried me down the hallway to their bedroom. A few minutes later Miss Flossie came in the front door with Miss Carolyn. Much of what happened next, I can't or won't remember. One thing I can recall was hearing Miss Flossie say that all the evil had to come out of me. It hurt when I walked. It hurt when I talked. It hurt when I sat down. It hurt when I opened my eyes. It hurt when my eyes were closed. I wanted to search for my pocketbook to see if I had one down there but I was too afraid to find out if it was gone. Some of it was still there because Miss Flossie and Big Mama were doing something to it. They said I would be scarred. My imaginary friend took me back to sleep. In between the prayers from Big Mama and the medicine from Miss Flossie, I knew that I did not want to move. Big Mama said I had to. She said I had to get on the slop jar so that the evil would leave out of me.

Big Mama's slop jar is in the corner of the room and they moved me over to it. Normally she does not let anyone use it. She says her personal business is her business. I did not want the evil in me. Not knowing exactly what it was, but it did not feel good. I was ready for it to be gone. So, I peed. It hurt when I peed. It burned, and I figured that it was what evil did. It burned you. It hurt you. It scarred you. Evil had burned my pocketbook. I cried as the fire from it burst forth from the place my pocketbook had been. I fell asleep again. When I woke up I still couldn't move. I had lost the green frog. I had lost my pocketbook. I had lost Imogene.

I was in Big Mama's bed. When she came back into the room she had a big pan. Reaching into her chifforobe, she grabbed an old bottle with a discolored and tattered label. Opening it, she poured some smelly looking water in the pan and slid it under the bed. She told me that it was some turpentine. She said that it would take all the soreness from my body and make me feel better. I was happy to hear that. Take the soreness and the evil please. Again, I asked Him to be my friend and take the evil out of me. He never said if He would or if He would not.
Somebody was knocking on the door. I was lying on the quilt that Big Mama kept folded at the foot of her bed. She had never let me lay on it before. She said too many souls had been threaded into it. It was the way she said it that let me know not to ask

questions. I would ask Lil Bruh and he would just tell me that Big Mama talks crazy sometimes. But I felt so much better with those souls covering me.

When Miss Carolyn came into the room I pretended to be asleep. I don't know why. I just did. I knew something bad had happened and I didn't want to talk. I had been a bad girl. I felt bad inside. I should have stopped counting them old stupid numbers and stayed by the back door of Mr. Robert's store. I thought that if she looked at me she could tell that I had evil inside of me. She dropped down on the side of the bed, glancing over at me and began to cry. Big Mama hushed her and they left to go outside the room to talk. I was so hungry. Because of the green frog I never eaten my honey bun, my cheese or vienna sausages. He had messed up my whole day. After a while I stopped pretending and fell asleep.

I heard people talking when I woke up. They were saying that I could die. Somebody else said that I wouldn't be the only one. I was trying to make out what was said. It sounded all jumbled up. Then it got quiet. But I think Miss Flossie said that they couldn't take me to the horse pit, and if they did Lil Bruh would be sent to be with the gang. It didn't make any sense to me. My imaginary friend took me back to sleep.

I slid off the bed and almost fell. It was a long way to the floor and I had forgotten how tall Big Mama's bed was. But I had to pee. My legs were still hurting, but I wanted that burning evil out of me. I had rags between my legs and I couldn't untie the knots. I moved the lid from the slop jar and the noise of it hitting the floor brought Big Mama running in the room. I had tried to crawl over to it and now I was peeing on Big Mama's floor. The only thing left to do was cry. She wasn't even mad though. Big Mama just kept calling His name and this time I did too. Maybe He was asleep because He never said anything to me. Maybe He did not want to be my friend. All I knew, I was laying on the floor in a puddle of pee with bloody rags between my legs and a smelly towel tied around me. I don't think that Big Mama knew Him like she thought she did.

How in the world could He let this happen to me? I was always a good little girl. Didn't He know that? Couldn't He see? Why am I trying to talk with Him anyway? It was stupid trying to talk to somebody who wasn't even available anyway. I will just keep my own friends. They talk to me, and I don't have to beg them either.

Some days passed and I was able to get up without falling. Lil Bruh and Big Mama would not let me out of their sight. Since the frog had tricked me, several times I would see them watching me with tears in their eyes. Lil Bruh was mad at somebody because he didn't tell jokes or tickle me. Maybe it was because of the rags he had tied around his hands. Big Mama would pour some of the turpentine over his hands and put some spider webs on them before tying them back up again. He didn't cry like I did.

Miss Carolyn would come over and sit on the settee for hours. Why didn't they do that when they were watching the stories? They would be talking and as soon as I came into the room, they would just whisper. I knew that it meant for me to speak to Miss Carolyn and keep on walking. Children can not be sitting in the room when grown folks were having a conversation. I was used to it. But lately all they did was whisper and send me out of the room. I made my way to sit on the front porch and count. Little by little I had stopped wearing the rags. My thighs were chafed, and my pocketbook was still sore, but it didn't hurt as much when I peed. The evil was leaving. Yes, my pocketbook was still there. Every time that Miss Flossie came and looked at it, she said that it was looking better and better. Time will tell, would be her reply when Big Mama asked her stuff about me. I wish somebody would tell me something.

I knew that it was about to be some more changes. My friends told me things, and tried to show me pictures. But they would snatch them away quickly before I could see them clearly. They never behaved like this before. So now they are acting funny too.

Somebody was in trouble because Ira and J.C. were sitting at the kitchen table with Lil Bruh. I don't know what they were talking about, but I know it was not good. They smiled at me when they saw me. I can still remember the look on their faces. They were smiling with their lips, but it didn't go near their eyes. It's funny the things you remember. I could tell that they were sad too. Everybody looked sad. They made a spot at the table for me and asked about the day we went fishing. I told them how many steps it took to get to the wash house. I could remember how long it took for us to get from the sidewalk in front of the boarding house to the red light. They were impressed that I could count to one hundred. I told them I had to count to one hundred for two times before we got to Mr. Robert's store from the railroad track. But I didn't remember anything else. They looked at me as if my head was on backwards. Ira said that it was alright. J.C. said that I was a good girl.

I asked Lil Bruh for something to eat and if I could have some ginger ale. Tears started sliding down Lil Bruh's face again, and suddenly he got up from the kitchen table. I heard the screen door slam as he went outside and sat on the porch. I heard the rocking chair hitting the wall all the way back in the kitchen and for once Big Mama did not yell at him to stop before he messed up her chairs. It got louder and louder until Ira followed him to the porch. Of course, now I'm confused.

I ate some soup and drank my ginger ale. Big Mama gave me another cup even before I had eaten all my soup. She had never done that before. Big Mama hugged me, kissed me and told me to eat so that I could get stronger. She left me to go outside and talk to her sons and Lil Bruh. Miss Carolyn just sat there and watched me eat. She was sad too. She kept patting me on my back and telling me that she was sorry. Sorry for what? What had she done?

J.C. and Ira were talking a lot. I was happy to see them because I knew Big Mama misses them. When she is on the porch talking to HIM, she is always asking HIM to look after them. That's what mothers do I was told, but I wouldn't know about that. When I had finished eating, I was headed out of the front door when I heard Lil Bruh talking. He could hardly do so for crying. But I heard him say something that stopped me right where I was. He told them that if he had not gone back to get the ginger ale, none of this would have happened to me. He was telling them that after he bought our lunch that day, he had to go back in because he forgot my ginger ale. Ira was shaking his head and telling him to stop blaming himself. He kept crying and waving his hands. I noticed that the place where Big Mama had tied rags around them had turned colors. He needed some more spider webs.

My little ears were only hearing one thing, and understanding none of it. The ginger ale did it. Ginger ale put the evil inside of me? Lil Bruh said if he had not gone back for the ginger ale I would not be messed up and that they would not have had to come all the way down here. I hated green frogs and now I hated ginger ale. When he realized that I had heard him, Lil Bruh picked me up and held me so tight. There was that song again. It was the same thumping that I heard when he carried me from the alley behind the store. J. C. and Ira told him not to worry and that it was time to go. Time for who to go where? Lil Bruh put me down and Big Mama walked him out back to the shed. Why did I feel like I could not breathe? Again, I knew something was wrong. J.C. and Ira told me not to worry and that they would always take care of me. J.C. picked me up and hugged me too. After a few minutes, Ira beckoned for us to go back into the house. We passed the kitchen and made our way to the back porch.

I'm witnessing the strangest thing that I had ever seen in my life! Big Mama and Lil Bruh kissed and then hugged.

Sidebar: Showing affection and love were not generally seen in my family. The only time people did was at funerals. Big Mama would say that it was a shame that the only time most got together was when something bad happened and a loved one died. Seeing romantic love in action was pretty much obsolete. Most of the women were afraid to let it be known that they enjoyed sex. If they did they were considered nasty. Big Mama said that the bedroom and the bathroom were places where you got rid of stuff that the body didn't need.

Here we go, let's get back to it.......

Big Mama was touching Lil Bruh's face and he had his hands wrapped around her plaits. Yes, I knew beyond a shadow of a doubt that something was terribly wrong. I heard the fan humming in the kitchen window. I could smell the smoke from the pile of burning trash behind the shed. I felt the sticker briars underneath my feet as I scampered to the side of the shed. They stood embracing, crying, and touching. I could only stand there in silence. I was watching my known world crumble and I could do nothing about it. I wanted to hold on to Lil Bruh's hand. The place where Big Mama wrapped her love and her healing salts was turning red again. She placed her lips on them briefly and headed back into the house. Lil Bruh told me that he had to go back with Ira and J.C. to work for a while. He said he loved me and he made me promise to behave, to mind Big Mama, be a good girl, and help her until he came back home. He kept talking and I saw his lips moving, but I had closed my heart and my ears at the same time. All I knew was this; I had lost me, my pocketbook, and now Lil Bruh. I hated green frogs and I hated ginger ale.

CHAPTER 3

A LIE DON'T CARE WHO TELL IT

After Lil Bruh left we didn't go fishing anymore. He had been gone for a long time; at least it seemed like it to me. Miss Carolyn and Big Mama did not watch their stories as much either. We didn't go to Mr. Robert's store for pork chops or rutabagas. It was closed down anyway. They say he moved away after his son died. Fine with me, Mr. Robert was mean anyway. Big Mama did not sing as much, but she did talk to Him sometimes. She didn't laugh as often as she used to either. I guess He wasn't as funny to her anymore either since I heard her crying a lot more. Then again it might be because Lil Bruh wasn't there to make her laugh. She let me sleep with her sometimes and when I did I would wake up smelling like peppermint.

I had been going to school for a while. I loved reading. I would read everything that I could find. Not only did I love to read, I could draw. If I could see it, I could draw it. Big Mama said I had a gift. She said I had a gift and I would go a long way in life if I put my mind to it. Big Mama said folks without schooling would have a hard head, a hard heart, and a hard life. They would always be tired because they had to work with their back and not with their head. She made sure that I did well in school. It was easy for me because I enjoyed it so much. When I was younger Miss Carolyn walked me to school. She was going to Lady Ann's house. Lady Ann lived across the street from my school. She was the one who had bought the store that old mean Mr. Robert used to own. Lady Ann was nice to everybody. She would let anyone walk in the front door or the back door of her store. I never went through the back anyway. Lady Ann had hired Miss Carolyn to clean her house and to iron for her. Miss Carolyn loved it because she said Lady Ann's house was always clean when she got there.

I was about 12 years old when my class got another teacher. Her name was Miss. Helen Burrows. She hugged me as soon as I stood inside the door. She said that she was glad to meet me and I could not stop grinning. It was perfect.... for a little while. I felt special. Some of the other children liked me because I could draw so well. We would sit and color at recess and sometimes at lunch. I was growing up and getting taller. The P.E. coach asked me to play basketball. I asked Big Mama and she said she would pray about it.

One day after eating lunch we lined up to go back inside. Miss Burrows was talking with some other people down the hallway. Much later she introduced a new student to everyone. Her name was Delois Benson. She was so pretty. Delois was the color of the honey that Big Mama poured in the "Anything" bottle. That's what Big Mama called it. The "Anything" bottle had peppermint, castor oil, herbs, vinegar, honey, and her own special ingredient. I don't care what was wrong with you, she made you drink out of the "Anything" bottle. Big Mama said, "If it doesn't kill you, it will cure you." If I sneezed I had to drink it. If I coughed, stumped my toe, or if my head hurt, I had to drink some. I didn't like it because I always had to go to the bathroom whenever I would drink from the "Anything" bottle. I guess it got rid of something my body didn't need anyway.

Big Mama said that playing basketball would be good for me. She was always talking about I needed to be around some younger folk because I acted too old. How do you act old? Anyway, I had a good time at P.E. and I was pretty good. Nobody seemed to mind that I was ugly. I continued to draw, and I made good grades too. I noticed that Delois did not like her books. She would go to sleep in class and Miss Burrows would take her outside to talk. Whenever Delois came back in she looked like she had been crying. I took to her like we had been friends forever. We did everything together at school. She liked basketball too. We ate lunch together and before you knew it, she was bringing me snacks from home. I asked her why she was always sleepy in class, and she would just shrug and change the subject. My imaginary friends would whisper things, but I ignored them. Months passed and before you knew it, it was time for the holidays. Delois was sad and I cheered her up by drawing her.

The picture was of her and a family playing at the beach. She always talked about one day visiting the beach. This was a dream of hers. Running in the sand and jumping in the water. She surprised me and said that she had drawn me a picture too. She said it meant that we were friends for life. Smiling, she handed me a picture with a butterfly on it and said it didn't look as pretty as my drawing. It was so beautiful. She said that she knew I could draw well, but she wanted me to have this picture. It looked like the butterflies at the red barn. I knew that it was a sign. I was always getting signs and seeing stuff before it happened. I didn't say anything to anybody. I have learned that it wasn't normal to see and hear some of the things that I did. I kept it to myself and sometimes wrote it down. But that's another story.

I wanted to tell Delois. I wanted to tell her about the other pictures that I had "seen". But I didn't know how to bring it up. Before it was time to go home I made my way to her. I thanked her and she hugged me so hard. She waved goodbye to me and hurried outside. We only had 2 more days before we would get 2 ½ weeks off for Christmas. I watched Delois leave to go home and I saw her smile vanish when the man got out of the car and beckoned for her to get in. He frowned at me and sped off. I continued to smile and skipped on over to Lady Ann's house. Miss Carolyn had asked Big Mama if I could help her carry some things home after school.

That day I was waiting on Miss Carolyn to finish ironing Lady Ann's clothes. I was sitting back in the sunroom, minding my own business when I heard Miss Carolyn and Mr. James whispering. They were talking about Mr. Robert's son who had died years ago. Mr. James said it was a shame what had happened to him. He said everybody in Red Ash knew that white boy wasn't quite right in the head. Mr. James' friend was the man that drove the sick wagon, and he had told him that he could tell the boy was dead before he arrived at the hospital. He had been beaten almost unrecognizable. Mr. James told Miss Carolyn something else that got her so upset that she almost burned Lady Ann's blouse. She slammed the iron down while Mr. James kept on shaking his head. He was talking about how the light was about to bring out what had been in the dark. Miss Carolyn told him to be quiet. I couldn't hear everything, even though I was trying to. Mr. James said it probably was somebody Mr. Robert owed money to. Everybody knew he played the numbers and was in deep with the Mafia. I kept my eyes on my orange butterfly, but I was listening to what Mr. James was saying also. When Miss Carolyn looked up and saw me, she made me go outside. Now, I will never know what he said. I left the door open as I went out. I was used to having to leave when grown folk were talking. But there was something different this time. Suddenly, I smelled wet dirt. Splotches of green flashed before my eyes as sounds of someone running vibrated in my ears. It's happening again. The pictures are back.

Growing up, whenever Big Mama and Lil Bruh had company I had to go outside or back in my room. Whenever Mrs. Jewel and Sister Denise came to play pitty pat, I had to go outside. When Miss Carolyn came back from the store with Mr. James, I had to go outside. When Bubba and Jr., the men Lil Bruh used to work with brought a load of water to the shed, I had to go outside. Whenever the grown folks needed to say something I couldn't hear, I had to go outside. I was used to it, but this time, I felt a great desire to know what the whispers were about. I believed that it had to do with Lil Bruh moving to Atlanta to work. I couldn't prove it, but I believed it. My imaginary friend thought so too.

I went outside and sat at the table where Miss Carolyn folded the clothes as she took them off the line. I was still looking at the orange butterfly. It looked so familiar.
As Miss Carolyn and I walked home she was very quiet. That was unusual for her. Just as Lil Bruh had been known for laughing and Big Mama for singing, Miss Carolyn was known

for talking. The fact that she was not talking let me know something was wrong. I could tell that she was worried. I figured out that she was upset and mad at Mr. James. The wrinkling of her forehead with her tightly pressed lips sent a message that she was angry, and she was thinking. When we left Lady Ann's house, she did not even wave at him because the hand that was not holding the bag of groceries was clinched into a fist. Since she was always nice to him, he must have said something awful to make her furious. After all, Big Mama said he was the closest thing to the man on the horse and she better learn how to ride. I know he did not have a horse, so Big Mama was talking funny again. Whenever Big Mama said that, Miss Carolyn would shake her head and laugh, because she often talked about riding a horse. I never figured out why I had to leave out of the room because of a horse, but it never failed. However, today Miss Carolyn was not smiling, not waving, and not talking about riding a horse.

When we got to the yellow box Miss Carolyn came all the way up to the stoop. Big Mama was on the front porch smiling. I was so happy because she was happy. I skipped up to the top step and I smelled the aroma of her baking before I got on the porch. Big Mama made cakes for folks, especially around the holidays. I was already getting in the Christmas mood. It wasn't Christmas until I licked the spoon and ran my fingers on the inside of the mixing bowl.

Big Mama was dancing too. She had just read a letter from Lil Bruh. He was coming home soon. I jumped off the porch and ran around the house. I was so happy. I pranced all around the shed. I danced in the vegetable garden. I twirled in the clothes on the clothesline and hopped around the woodpile. I turned cartwheels on the sidewalk, and I beat on the old tin tub hanging outside on the back porch. That was my sign. I got the picture of the orange butterfly from Delois, and my Lil Bruh was coming home. He had been at work a long time. J.C. and Ira had not even been back for Mother's Day or Thanksgiving. At least we hadn't had any trouble either. By the time I ran back to the front yard and made it to Big Mama, she was sitting in the rocking chair with her head down. Miss Caroline had put the bags in one of the rocking chairs as she patted Big Mama's shoulders. Uh oh…..what now?

When she looked at me her eyes had the same look that Ira and J.C. had that night so long ago. This time she told me to go in the house and they stayed outside and talked. The old Miss Carolyn was back. She talked and talked and talked. I noticed that the orange butterfly was gone. I looked everywhere. I must have dropped it when I jumped off the porch. I went outside through the hallway towards the back porch. I didn't see it anywhere. As I made my way toward the hedges I could see where it had landed under the edge of the front porch. I crawled under the house to get it so that Big Mama and Miss Carolyn would not see me, thinking that I was trying to be grown and listen to them. I got my hand on the butterfly picture and just as I was about to back out from underneath the porch I heard Miss Carolyn tell Big Mama that Lil Bruh could not come back home right now. She said Mr. James had heard some things and it wasn't time. I don't know how long I sat under the house counting.

I did not wait on Big Mama to tell me about Lil Bruh. I crawled out and marched onto the front porch. Miss Carolyn was gone and only the smell of peppermint lingered. I called out to Big Mama and noticed that she was putting dirt in the huge flower pot. I asked her about Lil Bruh. She pulled me over to the flower pot. From her smock, she took some seeds from a packet. Carefully Big Mama dug a hole and pushed the seed in. Placing the dirt over the seed, she packed it and placed more dirt. Taking my hand, she led me in the house to the china cabinet. Inside the drawers of the cabinet were some pictures, her glass cat, and a brown box with papers. She said Lil Bruh is never coming back. Big Mama said Lil Bruh was buried like the seed she had planted. He is dead, buried, and can not be seen. Then she said everything in my heart, everything that I love, everything that matters to me I'm putting in this brown box. She told me that she was clearing a little seat in her heart for me and Jesus only. Big Mama told me that she couldn't hold anything else. She hugged me and left me standing there trying to figure out how the seed in the dirt and a seat in the heart would ever bring Lil Bruh home. My orange butterfly was crumpled in my hand. I had held it too tight as I listened to Big Mama. I didn't even notice it. I loved my butterfly picture but I ruined it because I held it too tightly. It was to be a lesson to me in years to come. Sometimes you just have to let things go, some things are not meant to be held.

Sidebar: There will be times that even the strongest person gets weak. When you are the one who everyone comes to for support, without having a leaning post or a prop, one day you will fall. One of the worst things that can happen is forgetting to fill up. As you attempt to drive, you realize that you are not going anywhere because you have run out of gas. I was taught by example. You better not ask for help either. Strong folk can't ask for help. They just wait on help to come or wait and die. Stop suffering in silence. Ask for help. Wait until help arrives. It's okay to not have it all together. Real strength comes from holding yourself together, and not always holding everybody and everything else.

Now, I felt terrible. I was sleepy and could not understand anything my teacher was saying. Last night had been awful. I couldn't rest. I was up watching Big Mama sleep. She had moved around in her bed all night. She was mad at her pillows and even kicked the souls to the floor. Finally, I just got in her bed.

I was sick. My stomach hurts. I felt my mouth filling up with water and I held my hand over my nose. Somebody was pushing my stomach up in my throat and I could not stop it. I made it to the slop jar just in time. Everything that was in me emptied. I tried to stop my stomach, but it moved harder against my hands. I felt so tired, but the pushing had stopped. I had to blow my nose. I washed my face and got back into bed. I was hot, my throat was itching, and I coughed a lot. In a few minutes, Big Mama was shaking me and telling me to go empty the slop jar. Morning had found me, but sleep did not. I slowly got ready for school and for once I didn't care if I went or not. I was combing my hair and I felt some bumps. They itched so bad I thought I was going to scratch my head off. I got the little red can with the silver top off Big Mama's dresser and rubbed some of the hair grease on my scalp.

I had to get to school so that I could tell Delois about her pictures and about the things my imaginary friends had told me about her. She would just have to listen to me. If she was really my forever friend, then she would not think that I was crazy. I could help her. I don't know how, but I would. But that's another story.

I talked nonstop to Miss Carolyn about everything. She kept looking at me with a small smile. Miss Carolyn said that she wanted me to enjoy being a young lady. She said a time was going to come and I was going to wish for these days. At that time, I doubted that very seriously. As I skipped into the school yard I felt so proud of myself. Today was going to be great. I didn't even feel sick anymore. Maybe HE was finally going to be my Friend too. I was going to be talk with my best friend Delois and maybe Jesus would come and talk to her too! What more could I ask for?

Excited, I worked as quickly as I could before recess. I had not seen Delois yet. Sometimes she comes to school late. I couldn't wait to talk to Delois. In the meantime, I was getting tired again. Because I had been up sick most of the night I was a little irritated. Still the excitement was battling against my fatigue. Since I had finished my work before everyone else, I put my head on my desk. I felt a hand on my shoulder as I opened my eyes to see Miss Helen staring at me. She looked at me kind of funny and asked me to come to her desk. Oh Lord, now I was in trouble. I felt so stupid, and it didn't help that my face and neck were itching now. It seemed as if every eye in the room was on me. Embarrassed, I had to walk up there and it seemed to take forever. Miss Helen asked me to come and go with her. Maybe I wasn't in trouble since she was smiling at me. I had never fallen asleep at school. She stood in the doorway and told the others to remain quiet. Before we got to the door of the girl's bathroom we heard the desks moving and somebody running and laughing. She kept on walking until we stopped in front of the sink. She asked me why I was sleepy and I told her because I had been up sick all night. She was very nice and let me wash my face. She asked me if I knew why Delois was not in school. I told her that I didn't really talk to her unless we were in school. I had no idea what happened to her. Miss Helen said Delois was sick too, and that she had been sleepy a lot.

She shared that Delois had moved away and would not be coming back to school. I was shocked. Not coming back to school? Why? I felt so sad. I felt like she was my only friend, real friend. The young folks at church didn't really talk to me, and that was the only place I really went. When Big Mama cooked on the weekends at the boarding house, sometimes I went. If she had a lot of greens to pick or corn to shuck, I would help. Big Mama taught me how to cook before I learned to tie my shoes. Seriously though, I could cook anything by the time I was 11 years old. Baked chicken, fried corn, lady finger peas, and hot water cornbread was the first meal I prepared by myself. Most of the time, I sat in the kitchen until she was through working. The children or young folk who stayed at the boarding house or visited when they came to town did not even see me. Even though we were the same color and went to the same church, I didn't fit in with them.

Miss Helen brought me back to reality, and her concern was real. She kept asking me questions about Delois. I didn't understand why she was acting so worried. I told her that the last day I had seen her is when she got in the car with her Dad. She hugged me again and thanked me for being a good student. When we got back to the classroom everyone was quiet. Someone had looked down the hallway to see when we were coming and they pretended to be working hard. Miss Helen knew that they were playing, but she told them how proud she was of them and thanked them for acting like young adults. I didn't know that she was making plans to come to see Big Mama. I didn't know she even knew where I lived.

The next day Miss Helen came to the house to see Big Mama. She did not stay long. I don't know what they talked about, because of course, I was outside. All I could hear was Big Mama rebuking, binding, and loosing. Now I'm laughing to myself as I remember my teacher running out of that house so fast. You would think she was running through hell with gasoline drawers on. I heard Big Mama say she didn't like stirring up no mess, because all it did was stink. Whatever Big Mama told Miss Helen was enough to make her apologize before leaving out that door.

The next morning, I got out of bed my face, arms, neck, and back had little blisters all over them. I took off running to Big Mama's room. What was happening to me now? I knew that I should not have been trying to eavesdrop. Now I was being punished. Big Mama looked at me and burst out laughing. I did not see one funny thing about this. I was itching, sweating, burning, and looking even uglier than usual. What was so funny? I heard Miss Carolyn call out to me and Big Mama met her on the porch. She told her that I had the chicken pox and would not be going to school. Miss Carolyn asked her if she wanted Mr. James to come take us to the chicken coop as soon as she got off work. Meanwhile she told Big Mama to give me some ginger ale. She must be crazy. I am never going to drink ginger ale. It had already cost me enough. Big Mama knew that too. I didn't know what a chicken coop had to do with the itching burning bumps, but if it helped I would be willing to give it a try. After Miss Carolyn left, I told Big Mama I would rather have the "Anything" bottle instead of ginger ale. She just looked at me. I didn't have to say anything else. I asked her why Miss Carolyn wanted us to go to the chicken coop. Big Mama said that my chicken pox would go away quicker if I let a chicken fly over my head. She said that her Madear had done this to her when she was little and it worked. I was tired of itching already, and I was willing to try anything. School vacation was about to start and it didn't look like I would be going to the Christmas play at church. But, I refused to drink any ginger ale. Lil Bruh had left because of ginger ale and I had not drunk any since.

Instead of Mr. James taking me to his chickens Big Mama covered me in some thick smelly pink lotion. I was so miserable that I almost told her to give me some ginger ale. I could not scratch anywhere. She said if I did I would have marks on me as if a chicken had pecked me. I could not go outside either. She said if the wind blew on me it would make the bumps go back inside of me and I would die. I could not comb my hair. The comb got tangled in the knots left from the scabs and bumps. I could not drink or eat without coughing. They were in my mouth and my throat. Big Mama said they were everywhere, and I mean they were everywhere. But after about 2 and a half weeks, which seemed like forever to me, I got better, and I was able to go back to school. I had one little mark beside my left ear to remind me that I had been through childhood ordeal of the chicken pox. I had other marks too but nobody could see them. The fact that I missed my best friend Delois was worse than me missing the play at the church. Big Mama tried to make it alright, but so much was missing. Even her big heart and big effort couldn't change how I felt. I knew it wasn't a Santa Claus because Big Mama told me about the real meaning of Christmas a long time ago. I remember that Lil Bruh said he wasn't about to work hard and let a little fat white man get the credit. I told you he was always saying funny stuff. I reminded him of the Santa Clause at the boarding house; he was black. He said that wasn't Santa Claus; it was Deacon Kevin. Everybody knew it was Deacon Kevin because he always smelled like chili. Lil Bruh said black or white, you better not be caught sneaking in our house, coming down a chimney or through the door. Big Mama told me that some things had happened to Lil Bruh when he was younger that made him dislike white people. I thought about it and I asked her if that was the same as Mr. Robert. Isn't it wrong to dislike someone because of their skin color? It should not matter who does the disliking, right? She just looked at me and never answered a word. She didn't have to say anything. I got one of those 'you must don't know who you are talking to before I knock you into the next week' looks.

A few months later while playing outside at Lady Ann's house I thought I saw Delois. It was just her face. She had on a big coat, and she was a lot fatter than before. It looked like her; at least it looked like the honey in the "Anything" bottle. I waved but she didn't wave back. She probably was hot. I still had to wear a T-shirt outside, but it was not cold. When the car pulled away from the school parking lot, I could have sworn it was her. But I guess not because the girl with the coat on was not smiling. Delois always smiled. So, I kept playing.

Mr. James and Miss Carolyn were the best of friends. She waved at him when we left, and he smiled at her. I guess they were good friends because I heard Miss Carolyn tell Big Mama that her horse had come and she had ridden it. They laughed for a long time. I went to the shed to eat my cookies thinking maybe one day the man on the horse would let me ride. I know I was tired of walking all the time. Since Lil Bruh left we walked everywhere. I really missed Lil Bruh. I noticed that Big Mama went to the mailbox almost every day with a letter. She must really be missing him too. Sometimes Mr. James would take us uptown when Miss Carolyn went to get her hair fixed. I wanted to ask him where his horse was but I didn't want them to know I had heard them talking about it.

I woke up and stretched my arms as wide and high as I could. Lately I was feeling tired and I slept a lot. Big Mama said it was probably getting time for my visitor, and she would tell me about her later. She said she was way overdue but it wasn't my fault. I was so glad that today was Saturday. I heard Big Mama playing her records and she was singing out loud. Big Mama was laughing again. I was going to clean my room and help Big Mama rearrange the furniture. This was my all time favorite thing to do. I loved to move things around and change the curtains and bedspreads. This was also the only day that Big Mama let me drink a little coffee. She said I couldn't drink too much because I would turn black. I didn't care. Just give me my coffee and let me dance. She would dance sometimes too and we would end up laughing on the floor. We had to be careful when we danced in the living room. Big Mama did not want her records scratched. She cleaned them with alcohol regularly and if it skipped a beat she would put a quarter on the arm and turn it up louder. I would arrange the album cover by the colors and Big Mama would take the records out and put them on the changer. Before you knew it, the room would be totally transformed. Big Mama said I had a knack for that and God was going to use my drawing and my other gifts to bless me and others. I was just excited that Big Mama was happy. She got that way occasionally. Whenever she had to go to Atlanta for her headaches, she always came home happier afterwards. In the days before her doctor's appointment Big Mama head be hurting her so bad that you can't say anything around her. Miss Carolyn always knew it too. She would tell Big Mama it's time for you to go to Atlanta and get your medicine so we can get along with you. Sure enough, whenever she came back her headache was gone and she was almost like the old Big Mama. We talked about Lil Bruh and she would go to the shed and sit for hours. I still miss him too. I never let her know that I would look in the brown box next to the glass cat to pull his picture out. I wish I could hear him laugh again.

A few days later I'm in the shed staring at my picture of the red barn and the butterflies. I know that I've seen them before. I am almost certain. Even though Lil Bruh told me a hundred million times that it was just a picture in my head from an old magazine. I know that's not the only place I've seen it, but I don't know if it's a place for real or one that my imaginary friend has shown me. When I woke up I felt something warm and sticky on me. Feeling around I noticed that I had messed my clothes up. I have not peed to bed in a long time. Jumping up from the chair I grabbed the coverlet and ran to the house. When

I got to my room I saw that it wasn't pee, but it was blood. I had not seen blood between my legs since……since I don't know when. Things were just getting back sunny around here. Big Mama is going to be so mad at me. I don't know what happened. She's going to swear that I have been playing with little boys. She made a point almost every week for as long as I can remember telling me not to be playing with little boys, and that I better not let them touch my pocketbook. I was going to have to fix this. I took a bath and put some alcohol and witch hazel down there. I folded up some panties and stuck them inside my other panties. I threw the coverlet in the closet to take to school with me to get rid of later.

My stomach hurt so bad. I had not eaten too many cookies earlier because I had fallen asleep. I curled up in the bed and cried. I didn't hear Big Mama coming down the hall. She opened the door to say something and saw me crying. When she asked me what was wrong, I started to apologize. I told her that I was a good girl, and that I didn't let boys play with me. I didn't know where the blood came from and I promised her that I was telling the truth. I told her that I loved her and would never do anything to make her get mad and leave me. Finally, she realized what was going on, and guess what she did? She grabbed me, kissed me, apologized to me, and hugged me some more. For the next few minutes I found out about my "visitor" and how she was going to come see me every month for the next 40 years.

CHAPTER 4

Romans 5:3-4
3 Not only so, but we also glory in our sufferings, because we know that suffering produces perseverance; 4 perseverance, character; and character, hope.

One day Big Mama and I went to Lady Ann's store. She had the best ice cream and orange soda. I was in my last year of high school now. I had a few people I talked with, but I just didn't fit in with the crowd. I know that the things they seemed to be interested in I wasn't even curious about. I guess you could say that I lived a bit of a sheltered life, but I liked it. Big Mama was always trying to encourage me to be more involved with church, sports or music. I liked to read, draw, and sew. I enjoyed my own company, and I spent most of my time making plans and daydreaming.

We waited to get our treat and eventually it was our turn. I asked for the ice cream with the orange soda. The lady fixing it said she was out of orange soda. She said she could fix me a drink with root beer or ginger ale. As soon as she said it I looked at Big Mama. For some reason, I wanted to run out the store. It had been a long time since I saw pictures or smelled things, and I had been happy to keep it that way. Big Mama told me to choose something else. She sounded so calm, but she was squeezing my hand so tight that my ring was digging into my flesh. The lady kept going on and on about how it had been such a crowd in today. She was mentioning the big church revival and how so many people were coming in that she had run out of just about everything. I heard someone calling me. Suddenly, I saw a pool of purple water. Big Mama was talking to me and the lady behind the counter was asking her if I was alright. The next thing she did was the worst thing she did. She led me out the store through the back door.

She said I was looking like I needed some fresh air. What happened next remains a mystery. As soon as I stepped out of the back door, I saw the green frog. I saw the 2 hands that pulled my legs. The other hand was pulling me from the purple water. Instead my head went under the water. I went all the way to the bottom. I saw the purple water over my head. I closed my eyes again. The wet dirt was on my back. I felt the weight on my chest and I saw the thing. I saw the thing that stole my pocketbook. I saw Lil Bruh. I saw blood in the dirt. The next thing I knew Mr. James had put me in the backseat of his car. Big Mama was holding a cup of ice cream. Miss Carolyn was patting her hair down nervously and the lady who worked in the store came to the car and handed me a bottle of ginger ale.

It had been over 10 years since I lost me, my pocketbook, and Lil Bruh. I know why I lost Lil Bruh. Memories came flooding back. The purple water was washing over my mind making it clean and clear. I now know why he had to go to "work". I remembered why I hated green frogs and ginger ale. I remembered the evil that had crept inside of me. I knew why Big Mama had to get the evil out of me, and how long it took. I remembered her talking to Him and asking Him to take the evil, heal my body, and protect me. It was then that I had stopped talking to Him. I just gave up trying to get Him to be my Friend. He never answered me back anyway. J.C. and Ira are the ones who protected me. Big Mama and Miss Flossie healed me. Lil Bruh loved me. I knew why Mr. Robert's son died. I told Big Mama back then that I didn't want to talk about it. We never did. I still refused to talk. I had put Imogene Marie Jones in the flower pot with Lil Bruh a long time ago.

I had a job at the library. I was around 17 years old when I began to question some of the lies the enemy had told me about me. It kind of started one Saturday afternoon at the boarding house. Big Mama had showed out! Everybody from the church dinner was bragging on the meal she had prepared. One of the big shots, (that's what Miss Carolyn called them), came back into the kitchen with a group of ladies. She was dressed to the nines, and the other ladies with her were also. They were going on about the food and asking for the secrets of Big Mama's chicken dressing. As I was washing the sweet potatoes, I heard the big shot tell Big Mama that she was teaching me well to walk right in her footsteps. She said I was going to be cooking in this kitchen and teaching my daughters how to serve a delicious meal. Now here this well! I don't have anything against anyone who wants to grow up and cook, but that ain't me. I knew that I had other plans. I was starting to want more, and to hope for more. I was beginning to believe that I could have more. Big Mama just smiled, told them thank you, and kept cutting the corn off the cob. But in my heart, I knew that I would not be here at the boarding house frying no chicken for these fake folks for the next 40 years. I said fake because Miss Carolyn calls them fake. As the maid, she cleans their rooms during these conventions. Miss Carolyn be talking about how the folks be lying, skinning, and grinning. She says most of them don't have a pot to piss in, or a window to throw it out of. Miss Carolyn told Big Mama that they try to act like they are all that; knowing that they have spent their rent money and car payment to come and impress folk that don't even like them. But that's another story.

Big Mama was smiling more, and I even heard her singing to Him again. Big Mama said I was growing into a lady and she was very proud of me. On my paying job, I unloaded boxes from donations and other libraries. I never worked up front to help people with check out. Mr. Dryer did the schedule and work assignments. I enjoyed the back. I didn't have to talk with anyone. It was just me and the beloved books. Books were my friends. They didn't laugh at you. They didn't pretend to like you. They didn't tell your secrets. They didn't point at you and stare. They didn't treat you like you were dirty. They didn't abandon you. They didn't lie to you. Books never hurt you.

Mr. Dryer disliked me. From the very first time that he met me, I could tell that he didn't care for me. It's amazing how things turned out for me. He was the sponsor for the local library reading contest. Earlier in the year, it was announced on a flyer in the lunchroom, that whoever read the most books during a 90-day period, would receive a book bag filled with school supplies and a $25.00 gift certificate from Sears & Roebuck. Well, the first day of school, in the assembly, Mr. Dryer was called up to give the prize. When he called my name, and I stepped on the platform, he was visibly disturbed. I guess he expected Marie Jones to look like someone else. He asked the school officials to forgive him for leaving the book bag behind. He assured them that he would give it to me at a later date. I have never received it to this day. I know that it was a lot for some people to accept blacks and whites going to the same school. It had only been a few years ago that blacks attended separate schools from whites. Mr. Dryer had a problem with awarding me the prize because he still couldn't believe that blacks could perform as well as whites. Then here I come reading 55 books over the summer! Who would have figured that!

My name was announced over the intercom and my picture was taken by the school photographer. That was better than any supplies I could have ever been given. Shoot, I was about to graduate anyway. The twenty-five dollars would have been nice, but I had my allowance. Being recognized in this way was the best prize ever. To top it all off, I got a job working part-time at the library.

Big Mama let me keep half of whatever I made. She said that was enough for me to mess up. I wasn't messing it up. I was saving. I wanted me a sewing machine. I wanted some nice furniture. I wanted a bus ticket out of Red Ash.

I sat on the porch making my plans and deciding on where I would live and where I would work. I had bought an Atlanta newspaper on my way home from work. It was so exciting to see all the events that were happening all the time. I couldn't wait to get there. The wind blew some of the papers from my lap. As I ran to retrieve them I ended up on the other side of the porch. For some reason, I was drawn to the flower pot. There were so many flowers growing from the pot. They ran along the width of the porch and along the side of the house.

I had never paid much attention until now. I wondered which one was Lil Bruh. The dirt had covered the seed, but instead of killing it, the dirt protected it and nourished it. I wonder what Big Mama thought about that.

Every Wednesday the preacher from the church behind Miss Carolyn's house would come into the library. I would be in the back usually stamping the new cards or repairing any torn pages and covers. Often his two sons came with him. He would pick up some new books while dropping off some old ones; and invite us to church. I would always be polite but I knew I wasn't about to go inside of that church. I had enough of them church folk from the boarding house. I talked to HIM when I needed to, and that was often enough. Big Mama said that a new preacher had moved into town. She said that they were a lot different from the others. They were loud and stayed at the church all day on Sunday, sun up to sun down. Big Mama went sometimes when they had a singing or a revival. She said she got what she needed and every month when her check came; she faithfully sent her tithe, seed offerings, and benevolent fund. I told her about the preacher and his invites and she encouraged me to go see what it was about. I might, but I am not staying too long. It does not take all day for nobody to do nothing!

Fruit of the Spirit Church is what the sign in the front read. Pastor Jonathon O. Kelly was the senior pastor. The doors opened before I put my hands to push them. I was looking for a place to sit when a lady with white gloves and a long black dress tapped me on my shoulder. As I turned towards her I saw several people staring at me. Mr. James was one of them, and he waved at me. I waved back and quickly the lady led me to a seat. I slid down before anyone else could see me. I don't know what I was thinking. What in the world made me come in here? I don't know any of these people. I should have stayed my butt home and got ready for school tomorrow. My Sundays were always my preparation days. But instead I found myself sitting in the congregation of the FOS Church.

The music started playing and it sounded like some of the songs that Big Mama used to sing. I was patting my foot before I knew it. The lady singing the song sounded like the woman on the radio. They sang several songs and many people stood and clapped. I felt so happy, so light, and so free. It's hard to explain. How can a simple song and the beat of some music make me feel so differently? I was sitting down, but inside I was standing up. I couldn't wait to get home to tell Big Mama. I knew she would understand. She always loved music and singing. I listened to the preacher and he seemed to be talking to me. As he took his seat, the lady started to sing again. Something began tickling my inside. I don't know how else to say it. I felt a warmth come over my arms and in my hands. My entire body began to shake on the inside. I looked at my hands to see if they were changing colors because I felt them warming up. Something was happening to me and it was starting with my hands. They were red and I could see straight through them. As I held them up, they looked like my hands looked when I used to play with Lil Bruh's flashlight under the covers. Something made me lift my hands up. The lady kept singing and I kept shaking. Something made me hold my head up. I began to hum and the lady kept on singing. The purple water was coming and immediately I stopped shaking. My head was bowed. My arms fell to my side. I looked around me to make sure that no one was looking at me. One of the young men who came to the library with the preacher was staring at me. He was standing on the front row to the left of the church. I was so embarrassed. Everyone else was still singing and clapping. It was as if whatever happened had never happened. I was sitting down with my hands clenched so tight that my nails had dug into my palms. Drops of blood fell on my skirt and I looked as my hands turned back to their normal color. When I looked back up, he was gone.
After the service was over, I almost ran out of the door. I didn't want to linger. Mr. James was coming behind me calling my name. I reluctantly stopped and turned to smile at him. The same young man was nervously waiting to shake my hand. He

introduced himself as Jacob Kelly. I muttered something and kept walking. When I touched his hand, a light flickered in my heart.

I didn't tell Big Mama about what happened. I didn't know how to explain it anyway. I did tell her about the music, and I tried to sing the song to her. She politely clapped and said I sounded wonderful. There was Big Mama talking funny again. After that experience, I started going to the church on Wednesdays. It was a little different from Sunday and I was sure that I did not want to go through that again.

Jacob and Jeremiah were the sons of the pastor. They started coming to the library to look at books and to speak to me. Well, at least Jeremiah talked. Jacob seemed shy like me. I was polite, but Big Mama had made sure that I didn't give boys any wrong ideas. I was not about to start now. The countdown was happening fast, I was getting ready to leave and live. Look out Atlanta! Here I come!

Wednesday came around again and as I made my way to the church I felt a little excitement. I found a seat and began to listen to Pastor Jonathon. He talked about forgiveness. According to him, healing comes with forgiveness. He said un-forgiveness is like a giant weight. When we forgive someone, the weight is taken off the shoulders of the person who has been done wrong. Forgiveness also removes the distance between us and God. He hears us when we pray and we can hear Him also. Is that why it was so hard for me to hear Him? So that's why I never heard Him. Un-forgiveness! Ha! I was angry. How in the world can He expect me to forgive those two hands? It was not my fault. I didn't do anything. This was too difficult; too hard for me. I know now that I should not have come. This was a trap. I closed my mind and my ears. I tried to ignore Pastor Kelly. He kept talking and I couldn't help but listen. I started talking back to him in my mind. I liked hating the hands. I was glad that they were punished. I already have peace and I don't need to think about this anymore. Again, it was if he was looking right at me, talking to me, preaching to me. I don't know how my heart came to be the topic of this bible study discussion. I'm not ready to forgive, and there's no sense in me listening to this. Yes Mr. Preacher, I bet you can talk about it easily. You've never gone through what I have. You don't know what it's like to be scared to close your eyes at night. You don't know the pain of feeling abandoned and unloved. You don't know the shame and guilt of knowing that someone touched you in places that you didn't know existed. How many hours have you spent trying to block out sounds and smells that made you physically sick? Where were you when my body was battered? My flesh torn? My mind seized? My love snatched? Forgive? I don't think so!

As if that wasn't enough, he started to talk about moving forward in life. No matter how painful things have been in your life, you can survive and succeed he said. Really? Why don't you come from behind that big wooden desk and say it to my face! You don't have a clue! Listen, I couldn't recall the last time I was so mad. I understood him to say that it was a choice, one that isn't easy, but necessary. I listened but I didn't agree with it. Evidently, he had never been hurt or harmed. I wanted to just get up and leave the church when he was talking about forgiveness. But that would have been rude. I still have to be nice. But I wasn't about to forgive anybody.

He kept talking and after a while I heard him. I mean I really heard him. Maybe he was right. It was time to move on. It was time to let it go. I wanted to, but I didn't think I was ready. Let me ask Him to help me. I hope it wasn't too late. I was leaving soon. I was going to Atlanta to school and follow my dream. I could sew and make a lot of money. I had dreams of designing clothes, and teaching others how to create beautiful pieces. I had saved a lot. I had enough for my own apartment. I didn't need a car. I couldn't drive anyway. Atlanta had everything that I would need. I was ready. I didn't want anything to keep me from moving forward and being successful though. He said holding on to the bad stuff will keep you from getting the good stuff. I had a lot on my mind. So, I decided to go home and pray. I needed some answers and for so much of my life, questions went unanswered. I made up my mind to give this Jesus a chance. I told Him that if He was real, that I was ready to listen. I wanted that kind of life. Free, loving, peaceful, and full of joy. I wanted to wake up and go to bed without feeling like I was losing before I started. I wanted to have meaningful relationships with my peers without them sniggling and shaking their heads. I wanted to meet a young man and share my goals and dreams while he shared his. I wanted to hug someone without feeling afraid that they would hurt me. I wanted to have a best friend who wouldn't leave me lonely.

I said goodnight to the lady with the gloves and stepped out into the warm night. The perfume from the flowers in the garden was heavy and it seemed to follow me. I smelled cigar smoke and exhaust from the tailpipes. I wasn't paying attention. I was the only one on the street. Normally the couple who lives next door to Miss Carolyn walks home after church. It wasn't a big deal though. I wasn't scared. The yellow box was just around the corner. All I had to do was follow the path next to the ditch by the railroad track. I had walked it plenty of times.

I skipped on down to the railroad track and was crossing the ditch when I heard somebody call my name. I didn't see anyone so I guess it was my imagination. I'm always hearing and seeing things! Good I didn't answer to it. Big Mama said when you hear your name called and you don't see anyone; it's the devil or the haints. I really had no desire to talk to any of them. I'm trying to figure out how to talk to HIM. Anyway, it sounded like it came from the direction of the boarding house. I kept walking and I heard my name called again.

This time when I looked I thought I saw someone. I walked backwards for a while trying to make out a figure. When I turned to start walking straight again, I ran right into a car. That's what it felt like. As if I had run into a car, or a car had run into me.

My chest was burning. My head was aching. My throat was hurting. I couldn't breathe. I wanted to talk but nothing came out. Before I knew it, I was screaming and yelling. I saw the hands again. Had they come back for me? Somebody please help me. There were two more hands. They held my arms over my head. The other two hands clawed my panties off. Where was my skirt? Why am I worrying about my skirt? I begin to cry and beg. Please don't. Please stop. They laughed. Yes, I'm sure it was laughter. Two hands grabbed my breast while the other hands grabbed my mouth. The two hands begin to beat my face, my neck and my chest. The hands tried to make me take the man part of itself into my mouth. Fiercely shaking my head, I refused. I saw me taking my last breath. It was suffocating me. Again, they held my legs. I thought they were going to break me apart. Please help me. My arms felt like they were being torn off. I don't understand what's happening. Because they could not position themselves between my legs, they are trying to turn me onto my stomach. With everything in me I am pushing, screaming, and praying! I am tired, almost gone. I tried to scream again. When that didn't work, evil reached in my throat to choke me. It was trying to get to my heart. I knew it, but there was nothing left in me. It was over. It had reached my heart. As soon as I had decided to give Him my heart, evil was going to get to it first.

All at once the purple water came. It was enough to cause my arm to fling forward. But the dark thing was leaving with my heart. At the last second, I pulled my heart out of his hands. I snatched it back just in time. My heart was torn. It was bleeding. But it was still beating, still living, more than I could say about myself. Even though I was dead I tried to stuff my heart back into my chest. I heard the ground complaining. It was arguing and groaning. Horses. I hear horses running. Was the man on the horse coming for me at last? I smelled peppermint and my friend who I had not seen in a very long time took me in the purple water.

When the purple water thrust me back from the quiet place I opened my eyes to see the snow. It was so white. Everywhere I looked it was white. Big Mama looked so worried, and when I saw her I began to weep. I was in a hospital. White bright lights everywhere; it wasn't snow. I barely opened my eyes and she was at my side. She rushed to the bed and began thanking Him. I had had enough! You're thanking Him at a time like this? I did not want to hear HIS name. I yelled at her to shut up. Please shut up. If you want to talk to Him go somewhere else. He never talks to me. He never listens to me. I never see Him. He never helps me. I'm sick of hearing about Him. He is not MY friend. Do you understand what almost happened to me? Did they tell you what I went through just now, as I'm leaving His so-called house?

Big Mama was shocked. I did not care. I was tired of being the nice girl. Being nice did nothing for me. I was tired of making the right decisions. I was sick of people expecting me to do what they wanted. I was worn out from being a good girl.

Sidebar:
As soon as you make up your mind and decide to live for God, the enemy gets even madder. You must realize that he is upset that you have chosen the Best. Getting discouraged when problems arise is not the answer. You need to know that it's the greatest opportunity to let God, people, and the enemy know that no matter what, you will trust God. Some people have the wrong idea that as the transformation occurs, and God begins to become even more real, that's when troubles disappear....no, trouble becomes greater. Remember this, adversity propels you to destiny. This is just a process that you must go through to get through. The enemy will use any un-submitted and willing vessel. This is the time to draw closer to Him. God is faithful.

Now, to my understanding, I had survived an attack from two drunken boarders. They had tried to rape me, but in the knick of time, Mr. James came by to rescue me. Because of my bruises and state of mind, I had to stay overnight in the hospital. Mr. James had been slipping to Miss Carolyn's house when he heard me scream. He had probably saved my life. Since I didn't die, I was going to live.

The next two weeks were very troublesome and demanding. The police came and asked questions. I answered them as best I could. They looked at me as if I was crazy. I don't blame them. I felt like I was about to lose my mind! They were in a hurry to leave the room and I was glad to see them leave. I wanted to be left alone. I asked the nurse when I could go home. My body was bruised and battered, but I was alive. I thought I had died. From the reports everyone had given, it seemed like it was a miracle that I was still here. So, I guess that was two times I had fought to save myself, with Mr. James help.

Mr. James was going to Miss Carolyn's house and he almost stepped on me. It wouldn't be the first time somebody stepped on me. He said after he left the church, he had heard loud voices. He was running so fast to see who was calling for help that he almost stepped on me as he ran past. He said he couldn't make out the two men, but he did see some figures running off behind the wash house. There were no lights in this area because no one important lived down in this hole. The people who lived here liked it because the darkness covered up their dirty deeds.

The police were more interested in why Mr. James was walking over in the neighborhood when his car was parked at the church. They asked him a lot of questions. He told them that he heard the voices and didn't take time to go to the back of the church for his car. They didn't believe him. Eventually he had to tell them that he was already in the area because he had a friend who lived nearby. He was going to visit Miss Carolyn. He didn't want anyone to know because he was a deacon at the church, and he and Miss Carolyn were not married.

She said she would not marry him. It would cause her to lose her dead husband's railroad pension and that was out of the question. So instead of marrying, they had been messing around for over 10 years. At about that minute I was glad that they were sneaking around. If he had not come along last Wednesday I would not be here, or at least not in as good as shape as I was in. Thank you, Mr. James! He's the only one I'm thanking. Big Mama is upset at me but I really don't care. In a few months, I would be leaving here. Red Ash, Georgia wouldn't owe me a thing. I wouldn't owe her a thing either. She had taken everything from me. Red Ash had taken my beginning and kept it a secret. For all she cared I didn't even exist. I didn't have a birthday. I didn't even know how old I was. It was here in Red Ash that Imogene Marie Jones had been lost. Red Ash had taken my innocence. Red Ash had taken the possibilities of me having any meaningful relationships. Imogene had lost herself, her pocketbook, her Lil Bruh, and Delois Benson.

CHAPTER 5

Ps. 139:12 Even the darkness is not dark to You, And the night is as bright as the day. Darkness and light are alike to You.

I walked past the row of chairs with the distinguished men and women who taught at our local high school. It was my time. I was leaving. I didn't feel any sense of pride. It was just another day. I wasn't excited about the phony piece of paper in my hand. They said the real diplomas would be mailed. I did not care if they mailed them or not. I knew what I had earned, and what I had accomplished. I saw Big Mama, Miss Carolyn, and Mr. James standing and waving. Someone was sitting next to them but I couldn't see well. My eyes were a little blurry from the bright lights and the overhead fans blowing. I was not about to cry. Cry for what? I was almost free. As I left the platform I realized even more how empty my life was. I didn't have any real friends, just people I went to several classes with. I was always a loner. I could never fit in with any one. Sports seemed silly. Band didn't interest me. I already knew how to cook. I taught myself how to sew. Home economics was a waste of time. I had lived a somewhat sheltered life, by choice. I didn't go out. I never went to a dance. I wasn't interested in movies. All I really had was Big Mama, Miss Carolyn, and Mr. James. That is not normal for an 18-year-old young woman, ugly or not. Anyway, I was going to live my life and have fun. I saw plenty of ugly girls who had boyfriends. When I got to Atlanta I was going to finally be happy. I only cared about me, my own apartment, my sewing machine, and finding a nice boyfriend. Yes, it's all about me.

After the ceremony was over, I left the area as friends and relatives met to greet my classmates. I was anxious to get going. Big Mama hugged me so tight and she was smiling hard through her tears of joy. I knew that she loved me. I knew that she worried about me too. But I am a grown woman now. I have stayed under her wings long enough. I've got to make my own way. When Mr. James and Miss Carolyn came forward to hug me they had presents with them. I felt special. It was a terrific feeling.

We were walking to Mr. James car when Jacob and Jeremiah came up to me. I was so nervous. I did not want to look at them. I had not been back to the church since my attack. I was never going back there either. The closer they got to me, the harder is was to breathe. I made myself be still. Hush girl and be quiet. You want people to think you're crazy for real? Jeremiah was about to become a senior, and Jacob had graduated two years ago, before they moved here. They greeted me and offered congratulations. Jeremiah said that they were just in the neighborhood, and winked at Jacob.

It took forever for my heart to slow down. I was so embarrassed. I know they could hear my heart. Marie! Please! Stop it. They are human just like you. They are not going to eat you. They put their pants on one leg at a time too! So, my ears are throbbing and sweat is popping up everywhere. Calm down girl.

Jacob and Jeremiah were very sweet. Jacob offered a gift and Jeremiah offered his hand. I accepted and said thank you. I couldn't look in their eyes, so I found a spot right on the tip of their noses. I think Jacob was uncomfortable too. We didn't say a word to each other until Big Mama invited them over for ice cream and cake.

Was she out of her mind? Really? I know she had fallen and bumped her head. As I was trying to come up with an excuse for them to refuse, they nodded and agreed to meet us in a few minutes.

My soul had departed from my body. This cannot be happening. I had to talk to HIM. I had to find out why HE did not like me. Why would HE do this to me? I know Big Mama is crazy, but this is beyond even her. There is no way I can sit in a room with no boys. Especially cute boys. Especially church boys. Especially boys who knew what had happened to me! Especially one that I had a crush on! Was this some idea of a joke?

Big Mama has been trying to get me to talk to somebody about my feelings. Ha! I don't need to talk. I don't need nobody. I don't have no feelings. I am dead. I am a nobody. What was there to talk about? She couldn't understand why I liked to stay in my room or at the most sit on the porch alone. I didn't trust people.

Everyone already had ideas about you. They identified you by what you had gone through, not by who you were. When people referred to me, it was to mention the girl who was raped by the crazy white boy when she was a little girl, or the girl who would never have children because she was tore up down there, or the girl who talks to herself and sees things, or the girl that nobody wanted to be around her because she was ugly, or the girl who is so dark-skinned that they keep her in the back of the library, or the girl who's uncles are in the mob, or the girl who had two men put their things in her mouth.

Can they see me for me? I knew that I had to get away from here. It would have to be a Jesus thing; a God move for anyone to be able to overlook my past. I wasn't about to give Red Ash any more time to take something else. Oh my, now where did the Jesus thing come from?

It wasn't Saturday yet, but Big Mama put some records on the record player. It's not everyday that your only daughter graduates high school she said! We all sat on the porch and ate ice cream. Nobody was saying a word. I couldn't read Jacob's expression. He sat quietly and often looked at me and turned away quickly. Jeremiah was talking about church with Mr. James. I acted like I was not paying attention. It sounds like Jeremiah is going to be preaching soon. He was so amusing though. He told Mr. James little stories and Big Mama joined in. It was on now. She could not let one occasion pass without talking about Him; in the church, at the boarding house, at Lady

Ann's, and anywhere else. Whenever Big Mama heard mention of Jesus, she would talk all day about Him. It was my graduation and I had to hear about how special HE was. HE was not so special to me. I mean HE never did anything for me. If it had not been for Lil Bruh and Big Mama I would be at the bottom of the river. HE was noticeably absent every time I needed HIM. HE didn't talk. I couldn't see HIM, and I didn't know HIM. Anyway, HE wants too much from a person. I can't give HIM forgiveness, so I will just give it a pass. I tried, I really tried. I get so tired of hearing about HIM. I was about to go and find out from Big Mama how long I had to sit and listen to this when I saw Jeremiah hunch Jacob on his side. What now? Jacob came and stood next to my rocking chair. He asked me if I felt like walking out in the yard. Not knowing what to really say, I said okay. I saw that he held an envelope in his hand as we made our way down the steps. He said it was for me and he wanted me to read it when I was alone. He asked me to meet him next Wednesday to talk about it. He started to explain more, and as I got halfway down the steps a car pulled up, honking the horn like a mad man. I watched as the person waved from the car. It was Lil Bruh!

I never touched the last three steps. I just appeared at the car. He opened the door and all I know is I almost knocked him over. He was laughing and it sounded so good. I heard Big Mama saying something about a surprise. The only man who had ever loved me was standing right in front of me. He was trying to look at me and I was burrowing my face further into his neck. I had memorized and practiced everything that I was going to say if I ever got an opportunity to let him know how much I missed him. I was going to tell him thank you. Thank you for picking me up. Thank you for carrying me. Thank you for loving me. I knew the sacrifices that he had made. I was going to let him know that I didn't blame him for the ginger ale. But when he finally pulled me back to look me over I could not say a thing. Not one word. All I could do was cry. My Lil Bruh was home.

For the next three days, HE must have changed HIS mind about being my friend. I was singing. I was talking to HIM. I had my Lil Bruh back. Maybe all the other stuff I lost would find me too. I know that Lil Bruh was MY surprise, but Big Mama said she was being treated too! She said she no longer had to go to Atlanta for her headache medicine! They just smiled and held hands. Big Mama was singing and Lil Bruh was telling jokes. The yellow box was shining very bright. The night Lil Bruh came back home, I didn't get a chance to finish my talk with Jacob. He and Jeremiah left after Big Mama introduced them to Lil Bruh. I'm grateful they came over. It was very considerate of them. In addition to that, having Lil Bruh home brought waves of positive emotions. I felt so much love. My heart is still in my chest. It keeps turning flips and dancing all over the place. I'm so glad I snatched it back.

I might walk to the church later to talk with Jacob. He seemed as if he wanted to tell me something so badly. Anyway, there would be time for that later. I was going to be here one more week, and I would hear what he had to say. Life was good! It would be interesting since he hardly talked. I don't know what happened to the envelope. I don't think that he ever handed it to me.

Happiness did not last long. Wednesday rolled around and I had had enough. I should have known that HE was going to start acting funny. I should have known that HE would switch out on me. It was bound to happen. Every since I have been in this world, the tennis match of life was always being played. Something good pops up, something bad volleys back. Back and forth. Back and forth.

I won't be able to start art school because my paperwork is incomplete. I can't believe it. Big Mama told me she mailed everything off months ago. When I asked her about it, she acts like she doesn't know what I'm talking about or how devastating this is! She said maybe God was protecting me from something. Now why would He start doing it now.

This is going to mess everything up. If I don't start school then I can't move to Atlanta. If I don't move to Atlanta, I can't sell my clothes. If I can't sell my clothes, I won't become successful. All my plans are just flying out of the window. I'm devastated. I just want to quit now. I can't take it anymore. That's it! It's over!

I know why I was born and I had served my purpose. I was made to suffer, to hurt, to cry, to be humiliated, and then die. This God stuff was just a big lie, a conspiracy to scare folks into doing something that they wouldn't otherwise do. So, this old guy with a long flowing beard sitting up in some clouds really was responsible for how awesome I am going to be. Ha! Stop the madness. I feel sorry for folks like Big Mama. They are caught in a web of carefully placed words and orchestrated moves and events that inevitably mean absolutely nothing. So, you all win. I give! You have proved your point to me. I am nothing. I will never have nothing. I will never be nothing. I can clearly understand that there isn't any value in me remaining in this world.

I walked to the back door and locked myself in the shed. I can't reach HIM. HE's left the building! Yes, it's me again. Nothing new, HE always skips out when I'm trying to get His attention, when I need HIM the most. I wasn't mad, just disappointed. I am used to disappointment. I am familiar with pain. I understand emptiness and nothingness. I have experienced helplessness all my life.

Listen, I'm not depressed. That would suggest that a possibility of hope exists. I know that it's a lost cause. I'm lost. I always have been. But I was beginning to believe, to hope differently. I must admit that I wanted it to be true. I had talks with myself. I told me that I was important. I figured I could be somebody. Just maybe! I might make something out of myself. Anytime I had a little bit of doubt, something always tapped my mind into thinking that one day I might be able to get up out of the hole. Have you ever wanted something so bad that you sacrificed everything you had to get it? What an awful price to pay, and all for nothing. How does it feel to get the box home and find that there is no prize in it? The joke is on me. I am the joke. Well, let me laugh with you please, but as always, it was too late! Tumbling into the darkness I rolled into a hole.

That hole has been here too long. You can never fill a hole up. A hole is greedy. It always wants something. Imogene had given the hole whatever it demanded. But it was never enough. Come on little ugly girl! The hole is calling. You better give the hole its due! I had figured out the hole a long time ago. If I didn't give it what it wanted, it would take it. I did not want to give it anything else.

If I could just talk to the hole and try to bargain with it I might be able to fix this. I stepped into the darkness. It was so quiet. The hole does not like light. It does not like air. It does not like water. The hole wants to stay cold, dark, hot, and empty. The hole was bigger and darker than I remember. It had been a while since we talked. Yes, at least the hole talks back to me. I just wanted to talk. I just wanted to understand. Why was it always so hard for me? Why did nothing ever go right for me? Why did I not have any friends? Why was I always alone? Why did people think I was crazy? Or strange? Why couldn't I be happy for once?

But I realized the hole was doing all the talking. The hole was louder than before. You can have anything you want. I have everything you need. You will never lose anything else. I understand you. I know you. Aren't you tired? Go to sleep. I know you need to rest. I have a gift for you. If you stay with me, you can hurt those who hurt you. They are here with me. You can make them pay. You can fight them back. You can make them listen. Nobody listens to you where you are right now. Nobody knows that you are even alive. You don't matter to anyone but me. You belong with me. You don't have to do a thing. Just go to sleep. Come on and let me cover you. The hole was getting comfortable.

Once I got comfortable, I saw the Hands. It had been a long time, but I recognized them. I was walking back into the quiet place. The purple water was pouring. I felt so good. I felt so light. This was what I needed. The sound of the water was playing a song. The melody was beautiful. I began to hum. Big Mama had never sung like this before. This was a new song. It sounded like a lot of people were humming. One voice was different. It sounded like the lady at Pastor Jonathon's church. I knew the song even though I had never heard it before.

The purple water washed over my feet. It was rising higher. Every place on my body that the water touched turned purple. I smelled a fragrance I had never smelled before. It enveloped me. The smell moved into my nostrils. I tasted it. It tasted like sunshine and cotton candy. At least what I think sunshine would taste like if you could taste it. It wrapped my heart with purple strips of something that looked liked cotton. How can cotton be so strong? My heart was no longer torn. It was fixed. Thank you. I had never felt so clean. I had never felt so sweet. I had never felt satisfied. Is this what pretty feels like? Something whispered in the purple water. This is whole. You are whole. I touched my knees and my hands passed through them. I started to laugh. The purple water was washing my shoulders. I could lift my arms above my head without pain. I recalled lifting my hands like this at the church. Wash me. Clean me. Make me whole. Who said that? The singing became louder. Wrap me up. The voices sounded different, but the water was still purple. It was washing my hair. The water was over my head now. I could taste it. It was sweet and cold. It felt cold travelling inside my mouth, down my throat. But warm on the outside. I touched the inside of my mouth. I realized I could taste. I could swallow. All of a sudden, the water subsided. I was floating away from the quiet place. I didn't hear the humming anymore. Why did the music stop? The Hands moved back in the quiet place. I smelled peppermint.

Big Mama was howling as she paced the floor. She was mad at somebody. She looked so angry. I know she was not talking to HIM. Whoever she was talking to was really in trouble. She demanded they release, commanded them to let her go, and told them in no uncertain terms to leave and never come back. She was putting the blood of Jesus everywhere. Whoever had made her mad had taken something from her. I heard her tell them to give it back right now. HE was there too. She was calling HIS name. Lil Bruh was washing my face. He was crying. Wow. Twice I saw him cry. Each time it was after the purple water had come. Did the purple water make Lil Bruh cry? I'll ask him later. I was too sleepy. I was tired. The purple water was gone and the black hole was too.

CHAPTER 6

Time is filled with swift transition.....

It was 2:08 a.m. when the Greyhound Bus thundered around the curve. It was late. I was hoping that this was not an indication of how the rest of my trip would be. I had been waiting for this moment for as long as I could remember. That doesn't really mean much because I tended to forget a lot. At least I try to. Still, I have been anticipating this move. Big Mama wanted me to stay in Red Ash. She thought with Lil Bruh home I was going to change my mind. As much as I missed him, I had to go. He understood.

The swooshing sound the bus makes as it comes to a stop caused me to giggle. Sounds like Lil Bruh made when he has chowed down on Big Mama's cabbages and butterbeans. I had asked them not to stay until the bus arrived. But they insisted on staying with me. Every since the bottle of aspirin from the shed's medicine cabinet found its way to my stomach, Big Mama fusses over me too much. It won't happen again. I know that. Don't ask me to explain, but I just know that. I had felt so desperate. I could not find one reason why I should continue living. In the shed that day, I was reminded how empty I was, and how hopeless I felt. It was a moment to come to terms with my existence. That's what it was, existence. But something happened afterwards. I made up my mind to live. I wanted life. I wanted to experience, and not just exist. Knowing that I came so very close to never having it, it had become my utmost desire to live.

As we waited for the bus to come, we talked about nothing and everything. You know how you skirt around important stuff and try to concentrate on the things that don't matter. I knew that I was leaving a lot of things behind, but I refused to explain. Inside the bus station we sat in the little chairs and watched television. I put some coins in the little set in front of us. We laughed as Hoss and Little Joe were trying to get the attention of the pretty girl. Adam got her in the end anyway.

We all knew what I was trying to do. Avoid talking about my feelings. I had not yet accomplished that feat yet. It was still easier not to say what needed to be said. You ever wanted to say something but you didn't know how to say it without hurting somebody's feelings? You know, when it's not a good thing or a bad thing, but either way it's going to end up being a difficult thing? It's like no matter what you say or do, somebody is going to be hurt, mad, or offended. So instead of saying anything you just hold it in. My mind was getting crowded with my words and other people's too. I was going to find a way to release and get rid of the extra. It was going to take time. But I knew that the time had to come soon. It was necessary. I was full of other people's words. I had them coming out of my you-know-what. I had been taught to be nice all of my life and now when I needed to just talk I couldn't. It seemed that I equated being nice with being a doormat, a pushover, weak, and quiet. The people that I loved more than I loved myself were standing in front of me and I could not talk to them. I felt so bad because I needed them to know how much they meant to me. I wasn't leaving them. I was leaving memories and events. I was smothered and trapped in my own mind. I existed to please others. I thought it was the least I could do because they had done so much for me. I had to pay them back for saving my life. It was funny. For a life that was worthless, I sure had paid a lot. Well the bank was closed. I didn't owe anyone anything else. But I didn't know how to express this without hurting their feelings. So, I said nothing. I tickled Lil Bruh and held Big Mama's hands until the last person in line was tying the little tags on the suitcases. We held each other and said a lot without saying anything. I knew what they didn't say, and I had to believe that they did too. Big Mama began to walk away. I heard her singing. She had already prayed over me before we left the yellow box. Lil Bruh joined her and I turned from them to begin a new journey and adventure without them.

They lifted the gate under the bus and I set my sewing machine and clothes underneath. I handed the driver my little folder with the ticket in it. He named all the places we would stop along the way. If I didn't know any better I could have sworn the picture of the dog on the side of the bus smiled at me. Nope, it's just me. I had long ago asked my imaginary friends to leave me alone. I looked at the dog again to make sure, and no smiles were present.

I should have eaten something earlier. But I was too excited. Big Mama fried me some chicken, cut me slices of pound cake and gave me a thermos with some RC cola. I put the greasy brown bag in my satchel and stepped up in the bus. I was on my way. They would see one day. I would show them. The next time they referred to me, I would be known as a winner. I was going to put Red Ash on the map.

My stomach felt funny, and I was glad there was a bathroom inside. This was the first time I had ridden the bus by myself. This was the first time I was out of Red Ash without Big Mama or Lil Bruh. I am grown. I had put this trip off for long enough. I was stronger. I had come through some rough spots and made it. I was determined to prove to them how smart I really was. There was nothing for me in Red Ash. I had no friends. Unless you count Jacob Kelly. He wasn't really a friend. He was pretty much the only one who talked to me other than Big Mama, Miss Carolyn, and Mr. James. I liked him.

I didn't want anyone to know what I had tried to do. I felt so ashamed and guilty. But I had to get out of that house. I knew in my heart that I would never try anything like that again. So, after I had the incident with the bottle of pills, I decided that before going to Atlanta, I would attend bible study and talk with Jacob. I never saw his letter again and I was interested in what he had to say.

Bible study was interesting, but I didn't see Jacob. I wanted to ask Jeremiah about him as I was leaving, but I didn't want to appear nosey. Some of them already had such negative ideas about me. So, I kept quiet and went on out of the door.

I had tried going back to that church on Sunday; and to some special events on Friday nights. Ooh weeee.... them folks a mess. They didn't want to sit by me. When I tried to attend the youth night, it was politely suggested that I would become bored talking with their daughters, that I would be a bit too wise for them. The wives warned their husbands that I was fast, and they had better not be caught talking to me. The old ladies talked about how I fixed my hair and wore my clothes. I brought a potluck dish, it wasn't touched and I decided to take it back home. I would just throw it in the ditch so that Big Mama would not go back down there raising sand. The one time I did share with a girl in the prayer group, the next week that I went back, everybody knew about it. No one from the church came by to see me when I was sick

I was ill for about a month. My "visitor" came and didn't know how to leave. I was tormented with cramps and fatigue. I didn't even sketch any clothing designs. I didn't want to do anything but lay in the bed with a hot water bottle on my back, and sip on my apple cider vinegar. Every morning and every night Big Mama would put her oil on my stomach and pray. I didn't stop her, but I figured it was a waste of time. She told me that she had enough faith for both of us. Anyway, after about a month, it stopped. Big Mama said sometimes it takes a while, but it always works out. Whatever makes you happy Big Mama, you go ahead and believe it.

I had listened to Miss Carolyn and Big Mama's advice about everything. Miss Carolyn was still waiting on the man on the horse. So, you know I did not pay her any attention. Mr. James and she were still special friends. So how was she going to advise me? Isn't that how it is? Somebody that don't know nothing, and ain't got nothing, trying to tell you how to get something. Well, I was nice and I listened. It went in one ear and right out the other. A man was the last thing on my mind. I don't need one, and I don't want one either. I already knew that stuff anyway. I watched television and I read books. Big Mama said always be a lady. A man wants a lady. She said it all the time. I could hear her giving me last minute instructions. "Don't run behind no man. Don't make everything easy for them. If he doesn't have no hard time getting you, he knows another man won't either", she said. "Don't play with no man money, and don't let no man move in with you. Don't give away no milk. Don't let no man put his hands on you. Lil Bruh and I been together over 35 years and he ain't never hit me. If a man is interested in you for something more than the bedroom, he will introduce you to his Mama and his sisters." I listened, but it didn't apply to me. With my looks, no man would ever want me anyway. He definitely wouldn't want me when he found out about my past. No, I'm good. Thanks anyway.

I had been in Atlanta for about eight months. Things were going well. Believe me I was one happy camper. I went to school during the day, worked as a nurse's aid at night, and I sold my clothes at the flea market during the weekend. After about three months I had found a roommate. Because I had returned my paperwork late, there was no housing available. I had saved my money, and to my surprise, every penny that Big Mama had ever kept from my paychecks had been put in a savings account. I was motivated to keep adding to it. I swore that I would never be without. I would never have to depend on anyone, and I would always be able to take care of myself.

My roommate, Catherine, worked as a teacher and we got along great. She was a little petite package of practicality, common sense, and integrity. She was very strong and efficient. I loved her so much. She was always complimenting me on my pretty skin. I thought that she was blind. When I figured out that she was sincere, I didn't know how to take it. She was like this in every way. She didn't play, but she would give you the shirt off her back. Catherine was the type who spoke her mind and didn't back down. She had lived on a farm and she said she was used to hard work. She would help anyone, and many times she was giving money to help someone at her church. She kept inviting me to visit and I kept telling her I would go one day. Big Mama wrote all the time asking me about coming to Red Ash to visit. I lied to her too.

CHAPTER 7

Everything That Look Good, Ain't Good!

I met Ray Baldwin Allen in Woolworth. I had been working there for a few months. It was part-time and very rewarding. I wanted to learn about business. I was prepared to work my way up. One day I was adjusting shirts on a table when he walked in. He was walking towards me smiling and I smiled back. He said hello Beautiful and it sounded as if he meant it. He smelled so good. Mmm.....just as I was about to say hello, I heard a voice behind me say, "Well hello to you handsome".

I was so embarrassed. The young lady flew into his arms laughing and they joined hands and walked away. That was close. I'm glad they didn't see my face. I had almost made a complete fool of myself. Hours later I finished what I started; making a fool out of me that is. As I was checking out my last customer for the day, he, Mr. Hello Beautiful, came down the aisle to my register. I closed the register without giving the change back to the customer in front of him. Now I would have to call the supervisor. I didn't like to hit the tend key. Management let me know from day one that too many of them on the register receipt did not look good at the end of the shift. I was trying to be cute and efficient, and ended up looking stupid. My supervisor came over to help and soon I was able to complete the transaction. After the supervisor went back into the office, I came face to face with the prettiest man I had ever seen. Yes, I said pretty. He smelled good too. He asked when I was getting off. I looked behind me before I answered. He smiled and pointed at me. I mumbled something to him before hurrying off.

As I walked to the bus stop he was there waiting. I didn't have a clue what to say or do. I was a twenty-something year old woman who had never talked to a man before. Could this be what had been missing from my life? I had graduated from art school. But I couldn't find the job I wanted. During the week, I worked part-time at a nursing home too. On the weekend, I had a table and rack at the flea market. I sold some of my designs and I would sell out most of the time. I had a few clients that I made specialty pieces for; like choirs, preachers, disco band members, and debutants. Money was green and I didn't discriminate. I was doing fairly well for the most part. Catherine and I got along great, and I even visited her church a few times. In the few years that I had been here in Atlanta, I had only been back to Red Ash about three times. I understood why J.C. and Ira hardly visited. Nothing had really changed. Don't get me wrong, I loved going there to see Big Mama and Lil Bruh, but I loved leaving Red Ash and coming back home too.

This beautiful specimen of manhood approached me as I made my way out of the building. Several female employees arriving to work greeted me as I stood next to him. They had never paid me any attention in the few months that I had been here. They burst out laughing as they entered and I turned towards him as if the smirks didn't bother me. I should have known better. Why would anyone like him look at anyone like me?

Two weeks later I got fired from Woolworth. Ray's girlfriend complained to management and lied to get me fired. She had been there longer than me and so they believed her. They didn't give me a chance to explain or respond. I was devastated. I had been trying to save money to afford a smaller apartment on my own. Catherine was getting serious with her boyfriend William and soon she would be moving. I had less than 6 months to find somewhere to live. This lease would be up and since I didn't have a job in my field, I was getting nervous.

Over dinner I mentioned it to Ray. He offered to lend me the money. But of course, I refused. I had only recently met him, and he was not my boyfriend. We were just friends. So, I asked for more hours at the nursing home and they approved them. I was so tired that for the next few weekends I didn't make it to the flea market. I started back "seeing". Imaginary friends were bringing back pictures. This is not the time. I have been happier than I have ever been in my life. These last few months I have lived. I had never known that someone else could sit for hours and talk about the things that interested me. Here was a man who listened, and I was learning to trust him. He was very thoughtful and observant. He noticed everything about me. He convinced me that my dark skin was delightful and that my smile was alluring. He would touch me without grimacing and I couldn't believe how lucky I was. Things were turning around for me.

In more ways than one, things were turning around for me. I got a job at Stitching Plus. It was a top of the line specialty shop for up and coming professionals. I loved it. Not only that, I was attending church regularly with Catherine. I was beginning to understand so much. The things that Big Mama used to say were making sense now. I was writing to her and explaining my feelings. She said that the next time I came home we would really sit down and talk. I was content. I don't need any pictures popping up. I ignored what I had seen.

Catherine's pastor was teaching about the abundant life. In the bible, John 10:10 reads, 'The thief cometh not, but for to steal, and to kill, and to destroy: I am come that they might have life, and that they might have it more abundantly.' I had asked HIM to let me live. I was so caught up in living the good life, that I almost missed the abundant life. I was tired of the thieves and liars taking and stealing from me. I had believed that having stuff and things would bring me happiness. I thought that living in a special neighborhood and driving an expensive car would add value to my life. I dreamed of being rich and successful so that folk would admire and accept me. But the TRUTH of the matter is abundant life has nothing to do with material things. It has nothing to do with clothes, jewelry, and money. Jesus meant that He wanted to give me Himself. He knew that if I had a relationship with Him, that I would have everything else that I needed. Of course, I wanted to have nice things, live well, and take great vacations. But I wanted to really know HIM too. Yes, things were turning around and looking up. Ray had started coming to see me frequently. He was getting restless and he kept asking me to get more serious. I made it clear to him that I would not have sex with him. I was waiting to get married. He said he understood and that was fine by him. Many times, he questioned my feelings, wanting to know if I loved him. I told him I needed time to think. At times, he acted a little hurt because he thought that I was not really interested in him. I was either busy working or I was with Catherine at the church. I couldn't believe that a man like him would love me enough to wait on marriage. He stopped pressuring me and we had some terrific times getting to know each other. I still couldn't get him to go to church with me, but he promised that the next time I asked him he would. I'm still waiting on the next time. That's okay. It took me a while to get here too. I'm patient. He didn't mind letting me know how much he needed me. He was calling me often wanting to know where I was. I thought that it was loving gesture. He really wanted to spend time with me. He was concerned about my safety and whereabouts. He cared.

Ray wanted me to meet his family. He said his mother wanted to meet me too. I told him I would think about it. I wanted to be sure. I wanted us to be like Lil Bruh and Big Mama. I wanted to be cherished and protected. I wanted to be careful. So, I told him that we should wait a while longer before we took a serious step of involving family. We had only been together about four months. He grabbed me by my arms tightly and pushed me against the wall. The clock on the wall fell and crashed to the floor. Catherine heard the noise and ran into the living room. Now she was a little petite thing, but she was not scared. She saw him pinning me against the wall and reached for her bat she kept inside her bedroom. She was swinging it wildly. I assured her we were only playing. My heart was beating so fast and I had trouble focusing for a minute. After calming Catherine, we went out and stood on the porch talking for a few minutes. Ray was so apologetic. He kept saying that he was sorry. He just

wanted me to understand how much he cared. He was falling in love with me! I was blown away! I could not believe that this handsome and smart young man would ever feel so strongly about someone like me. I told him that I loved him too.
So many great things were happening. I had a good job. I was making a lot of money. I was dating a wonderful guy. I joined the church. I even started singing in the choir.

I was another person altogether when the music started. I was changing. I knew it. I wrote Big Mama almost every week telling her about Ray and the church. She was so excited. Yes, I was becoming that better somebody.

I met Ray's mother a while later. She was very nice, but she didn't talk much. I shared a little about my job, and invited her to church. After the meal, I offered to help wash the dishes. She thanked me and we were done in a few minutes. She kept looking at me as if she wanted to say something, but she didn't. Ray left the house for a long time and I was getting sleepy. His mother still wasn't talking much, nodding a little herself, and by now I didn't know what else to say. Eventually he returned to drive me home. He seemed upset about something and I did not know why. I tried to reach out to him and he moved away from me. When we were almost to my house, he stopped the car to ask me why I disrespected his mother. I was puzzled. He said I disrespected his mother when I fell asleep. I told him we both had fallen asleep. Ray said I thought that I was better than his mother and treated her like dirt. I opened my mouth to explain again and the next thing I knew my head was hitting the window. He grabbed my left arm and twisted it until I begged him to stop. I could not understand what just happened. What did I do? I tried to talk to him. But he would not let me say a word. We just sat there in the car for a long time. I cried because I was so scared and hurt. All of a sudden, he started crying. I had only seen Lil Bruh cry and watching the man that I loved cry was dreadful. He cried because he was so sorry. He was crying because he really loved me. I know he did because he had bought me nice things, taken me to meet his mother, and we had never even had sex. Big Mama had taught me much about how men are different than women; his money, mother, and material things matter. You have to mean something to a man who will give you these three things she would say. That's why I know I had done something wrong. It was just a big misunderstanding. I have got to pray and ask the Lord to help me understand how things go. I was going to add Ray's name to the prayer list at church. Mine was already on there. I forgave him and I apologized for going to sleep on his mother. He drove me home, and I waited on the porch for a while to make sure Catherine was asleep. I did not want her to know that I had been crying. The next day I went to work and received the biggest bouquet of flowers that I had ever seen. All is well.

Catherine moved out earlier than expected. She and William got married. They wanted to do the right thing so they went to the pastor and he performed the service right after Sunday school. Catherine was so beautiful. We laughed about how ready she was to be the Mrs. Catherine said she was not going to burn much longer. She said an engagement ring, intentions, and a promise don't mean a thing without the "I do". William was a good man, but he was still a man. Catherine did not budge. No marriage. No sex. Ray thought that I was mimicking her, but she was only an example. I admired her faith and her strength.

It was a simple ceremony. Everyone was so happy for them. I appreciated the genuineness at this church. The people were always hugging you. There were lots of opportunities to make friends. It was a totally different experience from the one at The Fruits of the Spirit Church. This new church, Renovated and Renewed House of Prayer, with Pastor Billy Lee was incredible. Small groups gathered regularly to pray with each other. I was learning how to pray, how to talk to HIM and listen. The women met often just to talk. There were special days of prayer and learning about the bible, and to balance it there were fun activities too. The women would go to the movies and bowling every three months. Pastor Lee said we had to be seen in the community as a loving group of people. He believed that everybody should be able to tell somebody something about Jesus. I wasn't good on that part yet, but he said it was coming. He said everyone had a ministry, and that God was going to use me one day.

Sidebar: Ministry is defined as service. Everyone can serve. Anyone can tell about the goodness of Jesus. We all should have a personal testimony about the ways He has changed our life for the better. The ability to tell others about Jesus, who He is, and what He stands for, in the hopes to convert or win people to Jesus is called evangelism. This type of preacher may travel to share the gospel or good news based on scripture in the bible in many different places. You do not need special paper work, credentials, titles, or positions in the church to talk about Jesus.

Here we go again, let's continue.

My absolute favorite group or ministry, as Pastor Lee calls it is W.I.T.T. We're' In This Together. It's an evangelical group of overcomers. We learn through testimonies, the word of God, practical demonstrations, and life experiences that we are more alike than different. It was amazing to see people from all backgrounds and cultures meeting to work together to discover their purpose and responsibility. We learn about everything from hygiene to holiness. I taught them how to sew, and others brought in hobbies and crafts to produce creativity and explore other areas of imagination. Pastor Lee said our minds are rich with the things of God. We have to explore the regions of it by seeking God. He said many people discount what they see or hear because they don't understand it. I knew exactly what he was talking about. I was motivated to talk to one of the ministers about it when I gained enough courage. I am a witness that there is a lot more than what meets our natural eye. But now is not the time. I wasn't that comfortable yet.

I wanted Ray to go to church with me but he was always working. He worked all the time. He said he was going to buy me a new house and all the finer things. I did not complain about his work hours. I was busy at work and church too. Also, to tell you the truth, I was glad that he wasn't around too much. Distance was safer for me and my desire to be a woman of integrity and obedience. He didn't pressure me to have sex with him, and I took that as a sign from God that he was the one. Why else would he accept it so well and understand me?

I went by Woolworth for a few items before going to work. I wasn't mad at them anymore. They had great prices and besides that, because of how they treated me, I received more than I could have imagined anyway. While paying for my things I saw Ray's ex girlfriend. She stared at me for a long time. I walked towards the back of the store and she followed me. She said that she was looking at me to see if Ray had started beating my butt. She laughed and I ignored her and continued shopping. When people are unhappy they want to make others unhappy also. I couldn't figure her out. She was beautiful. She could probably have any man she wanted. I just shook my head and headed out of the store. I didn't realize that I had been in so long. I get carried away looking for items for our W.I.T.T. Ministry group. As I was leaving I saw that Ray was waiting for me. What a treat! I did not have to ride the bus. As soon as I jumped in the car he hit me. He hit me so hard that I could not hear what he was saying. The entire left side of my head felt like a huge balloon as if it had been over inflated. The bell ringing from a distance was all I could hear. Ray was gesturing angrily and I couldn't understand a word he was saying. I just closed my eyes and prayed.

He drove quickly out of the parking lot. As soon as he got to my home, he dragged me from the car. My hands were shaking so badly that I couldn't open my front door. He snatched the keys from me and pushed me inside. I was still holding the bags and when I stumbled over the threshold, they flew out of my hand.

Ray took off his belt and whipped me. My hearing was slowly returning and he was screaming and cursing. He said since you want to act like a child, I'll treat you like one. He told me to strip naked. I refused. Why did I do that? He tore my clothes off of me down to my panties and bra. Across my back, thighs, and my butt the belt collided. I don't know how many times he hit me. He was thoughtful enough not to touch my face. He beat me until I bled. I guess that's why he stopped. He was mad because my blood was staining his belt. I don't even know what I did. I didn't have to wonder long. As he cleaned his belt he told me that I better never go in Woolworth again and say anything to Ella. That was his ex-girlfriend's name. I was too scared to say anything, afraid of the next hit. He was walking to the door and the look on his face warned me that I had better not open my mouth. My voice was gone anyway. I didn't know it but I had cried out so as he beat me that I could only whisper. Gathering all the strength that was in me, I crawled to the door to lock it. As the sweat poured off me it felt like some angry bees were having a field day on my back. I had to make sense of this. Sitting in the dark room half naked, I came to the conclusion, that he had beat me because his girlfriend said I came to the store to pick at her. I cried myself to sleep.

More flowers were waiting on me when I got to work. I didn't even read the card. I didn't even take them home. I already knew what the words would read.

Sorry does not mean a thing to me. I heard the word sorry more than I heard my own name. I don't need another sorry. I need help. I need to figure out what I keep doing wrong. I am so stupid. I have got to do better. I can't keep making this man upset. I just need to pray and read my bible. God will tell me what to do. I am tired of messing up. Our marriage has to be one of peace, communication, and understanding.

Time moved on and our relationship got better. Ray went out of his way to make up for the things he had done to me. When he allowed me to explain, he was so sorry. He said he should have known that Ella was lying. She was nothing but a liar, among some other choice words. I stepped up my game and tried more than ever to show him how much I loved him without having sex. He seemed to finally believe me and our lives were brimming with happiness. I was a lucky woman.

Past experiences began to plague me. I began to catch glimpse of colors and lights. Muted voices floated around me in a warm sheet of gauze. Pictures and scenes of movies were stationed in front of me. I watched in silence until the last face left the screen. It was Big Mama and a face I had not seen since I was little girl rocking on the front porch. The woman had dark skin and a penetrating gaze that went right through me. I closed my eyes and when I opened them I saw this same beautiful woman holding a baby. Blood was dripping from the corners of her eyes and made puddles on the baby's chest. Abruptly, it all disappeared.

I couldn't shake the feeling that something terrible had happened, or was about to happen. But lately I have not been feeling my best. I wrote Big Mama about it. I told her it was a dream, but I knew that I wasn't asleep. I was catching a cold, and the medicine I was taking was probably responsible for what was happening to me. Hallucinations were common with even some over the counter drugs.

I'm so tired. I can't rid of this cold, and I ache all the time. I know it's because I don't eat right. I work so much and I don't take good care of myself. It has got to get better than this. My time is coming. It has to! I've been waiting all of my life for better.

Ray picked me up after church today. One of the Sisters had told me about an open house event. I convinced Ray to go with me. It was a cute little house. It was not very large, but just right for us. I knew we could never have children, and Ray already had two with someone else. So, I was really interested in purchasing it. There were several people already walking through. The real estate agent, Mr. Jessie Haynes was nice and answered my questions. Ray wasn't particularly impressed so he didn't talk much at all. As we were leaving Mr. Haynes gave us an application and his card. I talked excitedly all the way home. Wouldn't it be amazing if we could own this house? Wasn't it awesome that God was literally opening doors for us? Isn't it exciting to make plans for our future? Ray just listened and nodded. I was ecstatic! So much excitement and expectation! Pastor Lee had been preaching about expecting miracles all month. He said we had to prepare, get in position, and have faith. Wow, this church thing is something else!

I walked in the kitchen to fix our plates, still on cloud nine talking about the house. All of a sudden, I felt an explosion in my head. I stumbled over to the sink and Ray held a gun to my temple. He had hit me with it. Ray accused me of flirting with the realtor. He said I was a lying no good piece of trash. I don't know everything he said. I was so frightened. I was afraid to move. I was afraid to breathe. I was afraid to cough. I was paralyzed. I closed my eyes and began to pray. Not aloud. He hit me again and told me he was sending me back to hell. He was tired of putting up with my crazy. He made me open my mouth and as he pushed the gun down my throat I almost threw up. He snatched it out and I remember hitting the floor. My legs feel like rubber. I passed out.

My left eye was closed because his fist needed a place to rest. I guess he had got tired of hitting me. My right eye was closed because the dried tears held my lids captive. The salt in my mouth was a familiar seasoning. I had collected many tears there. They travelled a familiar path down my face. It wasn't a big deal to them. They landed in my lobe at times, if I could move my head. If I could move quickly. If I could move at all.
I opened my eyes to nothing. How long had I been on the floor? It was dark, but I could see the legs of the kitchen table. A torn piece of linoleum was visible because the table had been moved when I hit the floor. It was coming back to me. I was in my kitchen. I was not dead. I was not in hell, well almost, but not totally. I finally made it to a chair and sat down. All I could think about was the fact that I have got to get me a new rug. The hole was bigger now.

Ray had eaten and left his dirty plate on the counter. Was he gone? I am terrified. I'm scared to go and see if he's still in there. The worst feeling in the world is not being safe in your own home. I didn't know what to do. So, I didn't do anything. I sat there until I had to use the bathroom. I thought that I heard movement in the other room. Was he coming to finish me? Maybe he thought that he had killed me. I should have stayed on the floor. I was panic stricken. I didn't know what to do. I just sat on the toilet waiting on him to come in the bathroom and finish killing me. After a while I decided to get up. The sweat from my thighs stuck to the seat as I attempted to quietly remove myself from the toilet. The noise of the seat hitting the toilet bowl was so loud, and it spooked me. I waited for him to come rushing in again. I pulled my panties up and stood by the sink for a while. I grabbed my house coat hanging on the back of the door and put it on. When they found my body, I wanted to be covered.

Ray had beat me, ate my food, and left me. When I finally made my way to the living room, I looked out the window and his car was gone. I locked the door and began to pray.

A few days later I went to choir practice. When Brother Christopher and Sister Julie hugged me, I bit back a scream. These are some hugging folks but my back and the side of my head was still throbbing. Still, it is well. God is working it out for my good. That's what Pastor Lee says. I'm going to keep smiling and singing. They don't have to know my business. Anyway, I don't want them looking at Ray funny once he starts coming to church. I learned that the hard way. I made the mistake of telling Catherine about the time Ray slapped me. She continues to look at him suspiciously whenever they are in each other's company. I told her that she must get over the past since he loves me. She told me that just because you have forgiven someone, it doesn't mean that you have to be around them, laughing in their face. Catherine says it's the God in her that makes her tolerate him, but she does not believe that he is the one for me.

Sidebar: You have probably heard folk talk about the inability to forgive someone is like eating something poisonous and expecting the one whom harmed you to die. That's a great analogy. It's a lot more to it. Un-forgiveness leads to death for sure. It cancels your greatness and your future, and it also stifles your present. It paralyzes your inner man and it won't allow you to experience opportunities and possibilities to move forward. The contempt and bitterness that grows from harboring revenge and housing hatred prevents genuine love and affection from attaching to you. In order to forgive someone, you are not excusing their behavior. You are not forgetting. You are not accepting any blame. You do not have to restore the relationship. You do not have to ignore what happened. You do not have to trust them again.

There you have it. I know that I should never have opened my mouth. Catherine is stubborn and she cares so much about my wellbeing. Big Mama used to say that teeth and tongue will fall out sometimes. She said never let your right hand know what your left hand is doing. Once you forgive somebody for mistreating you, your family and friends might not. They will hold it against them for a long time. I figured from now on, if anything happens between me and Ray, I'll keep it between me and Jesus. My prayers were going forth. Yes, HE is going to fix Ray.

CHAPTER 8

Lamentations 3:54-58

54 Waters flowed over mine head; then I said, I am cut off. 55 I called upon thy name, O Lord, out of the low dungeon. 56 Thou hast heard my voice: hide not thine ear at my breathing, at my cry. 57 Thou drewest near in the day that I called upon thee: thou saidst, Fear not. 58 O Lord, thou hast pleaded the causes of my soul; thou hast redeemed my life.

Ray said I can't go to church any more. He says it cost too much money and I spend too much time over there. He used any and every excuse that he could to make me feel guilty. I loved going to church. I would sit in on the outreach, youth fellowship, and the women's ministry, even when I was not in W.I.T.T., choir practice, or bible study. I knew that he was up to something. He had started pressuring me to have sex with him again. I have been dreading this. He said since I won't give it to him, I must be having relations with the pastor. "Come on now", said the look on my face. I told him Pastor Lee was old enough to be my daddy. He slapped me. He said them older preachers are the worst ones, because they have been in the game longer. He kept talking about how they know how to play on them young and gullible females. I didn't say anything else because my lip was hurting. I can't even reason with him. He will hit me just because he can. But I'm praying harder than ever. Jesus, I need you to fix Ray now!

I just don't understand. Ray loves me so much. I know he does. He only wants me all to himself. I must try harder to prove to him that I truly love him only. I guess we need to go ahead and get married. Surely that would convince him. He will change then and we can get old together. He will believe that I only want to be with him.

I still can't figure out why he loves me anyway. He could be with any woman he wanted to. He said I belonged to him and if he couldn't have me then nobody would. I know that I don't deserve a good looking hard-working man like Ray. I can not mess this up again. I have got to get it right. Ray never talked about the incident with the gun. I didn't either. This time he didn't buy me any flowers. It didn't matter because we were getting along a lot better now. I know that gifts and flowers will not determine his love. I don't need flowers, I just need him.

Since I can't go to church right now, I need to talk to the pastor or one of the other ministers and let them know. This is so difficult. I really want to see my babies though. Pastor Lee had asked me to talk with a young group of ladies who were finding it difficult to accept the love of Jesus. They had suffered rejection and abuse from people that they trusted. It was hard for them to believe in a Jesus whom loved them enough to die for them. My introduction had evolved into so much more. We have workshops now on discovering our purpose and determining our destiny. The church sponsors activities to teach life skills and practical means of employment. God used my love for design to teach crafts and sewing. As a result, we have created costumes for the Divine Arts Ministry. They are always presenting skits, plays, and dances. The ladies and I have become so close. I call them my babies, and they call me Ma. They are determined to have me in their lives and they include me in significant events. I have never been accepted like this before. No hidden agendas. No hidden motives. I would miss my lights of joy. But I have to prove to Ray that I love him. It will all work out. Anyway, that's what Pastor Lee preached last week. I took good notes.

I know that this group is as close as I'll get to ever having any children. They have become a life line for me. I was floundering, drowning, about to touch the bottom. God sent Catherine to me, and then she was the bridge that my brokenness came over. I know that He had set me up. I yearned to give them love and make them feel special and needed. It turned out that everything I was pouring into them, and they were showering back into me.

I must find a way to tell Pastor Lee that I need a little break. I don't want to lie, but I have got to fix things with Ray without letting Pastor know what's really going on. It will only be temporary. I have to be responsible and handle my business. People won't understand why I put up with Ray. They don't understand that he shows his love differently. He's been through so much, and he needs me. Besides, some women don't have anyone to love them. At least I have a man. He helps me, and he accepts me for who I am. It's time that I be here for him.

I will surely miss singing. Whenever I find myself in that choir stand nothing else matters. I sing and smile until my face hurts. Sometimes I cry. It depends. I feel the electric jolts when I sing. That's what I call them. I guess being in the house with Big Mama all those years rubbed off on me. I float and I lose all tracks of time and space. Something holds my heartbeat and the shocks trickle to my toes. I am often out of breath and weak when it washes over me. It removes hurt. It distances chaos. When it blows against my skin, I capture it. I hold onto the tickle. I never want it to leave. I can't stop singing. I need to sing. The sisters call it worship. Whatever it is, I love it. I love Jesus.

Since last week I have been holding on to bible study. In church this past month, all I hear is everything is working for our good; my good. In my notes, I found Romans 8:28. I hold on to it. I live it. I walk it. It's the only thing keeping me from going insane. It has become real to me, not just a scripture on a piece of paper. They are not just words in a book. I am so grateful for Him not giving up on me.

I'll ride the bus over to the church and leave a note under the Pastor's study. I'll just slip in and slip right back out. Ray will never find out. I'll make it back home in no time at all. Besides he will probably work late again. I made it to the church parking lot. Ray was sitting in his car waiting on me. I didn't see him until it was too late. He got out of the car as I made it to the front door of the church. He was smiling, sort of, that old smile. I was shocked to see him. I thought to myself, my prayers must be working. He had been listening. All I really wanted was for Ray to come to church. I had visualized it so many times. In my version of the dream I would be sitting in the choir stand. Ray would come in and hear a compelling sermon. When Pastor Lee invited the lost and hurting people to the altar, Ray would walk up and give Pastor Lee his hand. He would tell the congregation how much he loved me. He would thank me for praying for him, and never losing hope in him. He would apologize for every bad thing that he had caused to happen to me. He would have a shiny diamond ring and ask me to marry him, right in front of everyone. People would be whispering about how lucky I was to have a man like him love me. We would live happily ever after.

Well, it didn't happen like I dreamed, but at least he was here. I foolishly grabbed his arm intending to walk into the church. He snatched me towards him so suddenly that my right shoe came off, twisting my ankle. He was so angry. I was so petrified. He reminded me that I disobeyed him again. He told me that I was never to come back to this church. I was explaining that I only came to let them know that I would be leaving. He didn't believe me. I begged him to hear me out. I tried to show him the note. He was furious. This was a nightmare, not a dream. He balled his fist up and punched me in my stomach right at the front door of the church. I almost collapsed. I was so nauseous, and I threw up. Why in the world would God allow this? Right now? At the church? I cried and I continued to try to tell him about the youth group, the ladies fellowship, the choir, and the prayer group. He wasn't hearing it. He called me stupid. He screamed, "You will never be anybody. You will never have anything. You just ain't no good. You are dumb. Nobody loves you. They don't like you, and they don't need you. They only want your money. They are using you. They laugh at you and talk about you. I'm the only one who wants you."

When he had hit me a few more times, he told me to go inside and tell them I would not be coming back. He said I had better get back home before he did. He would be waiting at my house. Ray said for me to get back home the same way I had got here. He promised me that he had more of what he just gave me. He took his belt off and hit me again to show me that he meant what he said. All of this right at HIS house. I was more shocked about WHERE it all went down more than the fact that my loving and caring man had just beat me again.

I don't want any more. I have had enough. I was afraid to go home. Why couldn't I do anything right? I was going to keep on until I was alone and lonely. Jesus, can you help me? Jesus, can you fix me? Jesus, I need you. Why won't you help? I have done everything that you ever asked me to. Haven't I?
I walked into the church with one broken heel and two buttons torn off my sweater. Making my way to the bathroom I couldn't even cry anymore. I felt so hopeless, so weak, and so afraid. What must I do to change this? I can't help how I look. I'm ugly, but I'm nice. I mean it's not my fault. I had nothing to do with how I was born. I'm so mad right now. My own Mother thought that I was too ugly to love, and I finally found someone to love me, and because I don't know how to treat a man, he's going to leave me too.

I don't know how long I sat on the toilet. I forgot that Ray had given me a time limit. I was replaying the terrible things he had said to me in the past year and a half. I sat and remembered how he had hit me many times for nothing. I counted the lies I had told co-workers and church members. Could anyone be so clumsy and fall that often? It's a sobering experience to be able to list way too many reasons why you should NOT be with someone. I recited 1 Corinthians 13 and found it impossible to see Ray in any of it. I figured that my suffering was justifiable and it was what I had to go through. Was it a regular part of "growing stronger in the Lord?" Persevering? Being patient? Trusting God? I mean if I understood it correctly, we all have to put up with things that we don't like, and what we can't change. I learned that a long time

ago. All of a sudden, as my feet began to grow numb, my heart began to feel less afraid. It was racing with anger and rage.
I was mad at Ray. I was mad at myself. I was mad at God. Sitting there in anguish I examined my life since I made up my mind to believe that Jesus loved me. He was supposed to protect me. I wanted revenge. Ask me what I wanted God to do for me now! I was expecting angels to come rescue me, brush all my cares away, erase scars, and then go beat Ray up. I was tired of waiting on God to fix him. I needed Jesus for myself. Finally, I knew it. I could see now. I needed fixing. I needed help. I had allowed fear to cripple me and put me in a cage. I never ventured out. I didn't want to be free. I was afraid to try to fly. It was easier to stay put and be miserable, than to attempt and fail. My mind was disorderly and chaotic. The ability to know what was right and what was wrong was bent and disfigured. I could aim, but I couldn't hit a target. Every life choice had been viewed through a dirty scope. I sat on the toilet, concluding that it was time to release some stuff. But I had made so many mistakes.

I feel so dirty. I messed up so many times. I heard fear talking again. I had finally done it this time! These people will turn their backs on me too. Ray was right. I was dumb. I couldn't do anything right. I was better off dead. No! I have to stop the madness. I can't keep going back and forth. Something told me to get up and go on to the office area. I knew that I had to let some stuff go, including Ray too. I don't know how long I stayed there. Releasing. Letting go. Crying. Praying. No one came in. God allowed me to spend this time with Him without interruption. Some time later, after regaining the use of my feet I made my way toward the offices.

I didn't feel a thing. No pain. No joy. No despair. No hope. Nothing, but something had changed. There was a difference, still something was missing. I was so close, but I know that I wasn't close enough. I suffered a shortage. I was still inadequate, and I knew that I required a charge, a deposit, or a push.

I didn't know that they were having a service. I heard Pastor Lee talking while some folk were clapping their hands. What is going on in here? I looked in one of the classrooms before reaching the pastor's study. I guess this is why nobody came to my rescue in the parking lot. They were all back here. Bishop Marcus and Minister Derrick were standing beside Pastor Lee. They were holding his arms up. Prophet Devery was sitting on a rock at Pastor's feet. It was a play. A small group of adults were present that I didn't recognize. They were all listening so intently. Some were laughing. A few were crying. I pressed to hear what was being said. Listening, I was mesmerized. I couldn't move. I know that I wasn't supposed to be in here. But something pressed me in my back and pushed me forward.

He was talking ABOUT me. Pastor Lee was telling them about me, but he didn't know it. He was talking about being bruised, broken, and battered. He was recalling frustrated moments of rejection and fear. I heard him as clear as a bell. He said, "Your life is tore up from the floor up and you need help. He was talking TO me. He was talking about being restored. He was talking about regaining hope. He said there is no such thing as giving up. I heard him encourage them as he encouraged me. I was paying attention. He said God loves you. He began to explain that love to them, to me. He said the devil lies to you. He wants you to give up. He creates situations to make you feel hopeless. But there is someone fighting with you, and for you. He said terrible things happen to many people and they continue to go down a road of wrong turns and mistakes. But God! He said but God doesn't care where we've been, what we did, or what was done to us. He said God's hands stretches to hold us and everything that belongs to us. He can wash us, love us, forgive us, fill us, and use us. He said don't believe the tricks, plots, schemes, and works of the devil. He's a deceiver. He twists things, and he wants us to live defeated. It's a part of his program. Often, he will use our past to gang up on us. One of his most successful schemes pits us against ourselves. When we fight against ourselves, we fight against our destiny. Don't give up, the fight is fixed. You must believe the report of the Lord. Satan has disrupted, derailed, and destroyed dreams. You exist, and that's all. You are just going along to get along. Then he said five words that jump-started my faith and permeated my soul. IT DOESN'T HAVE TO BE!

He was so right. This is why I felt guilty, embarrassed, useless, and dirty. The devil had lured me into a state of despair. He lulled me into accepting a lifestyle that was so far from the plan of God. However, I was so afraid to believe, to reach. What if I failed? What if I fell? I already had my mind made up. I had come to the conclusion that I got what I deserved. I didn't want to sing no more. I didn't want to pray no more. I didn't want to hope no more. The preacher man was talking to me. But I have my ears covered. Can't he see in the Spirit? That's what they call it. I've gone too far and done too much. I was contaminated and my part of me, yes, my part of me that caused me to exist, had been tampered with. There was evil in me that even His hands couldn't reach. Wasn't it? I had to stop this foolish church talk from going down in my soul. Ha ha ha…… I'm not listening. I'm not going to let Pastor Lee fool me again. Joy is not for my kind. No such thing as peace and love anyway. That's for them other folk. I got no business coming in here anyway. I have been doing alright just like I am. This faith and forgiveness thing is demanding, it requires too much. Right now, I don't have to go nowhere I don't want to. I don't want to go up. I don't want to go farther. I don't want to go higher. That's too much work, it takes hope. Hope is overrated. I'll settle for down. Down is ok. Down is suitable. Down is fine. What was I thinking anyway? Child please, down is home. I got no business trying to dream. I got no business looking for faith. Faith and Hope are going to do me like all the rest of them anyway. Let me get close to them and then they will turn their backs on me, laugh and throw me away too. I'm so crazy, right? Who does the preacher man see when he looks at me anyway? He doesn't know nothing about me.

Mad and upset, I needed to leave, but I kind of wanted to talk to Him. HE tricked me. I really didn't want to hear what HE had to say after all this time. But I had so many buried and forgotten questions. No, I didn't want to talk to Him. So instead I asked my long-time friend, Pain. I knew that Pain would never leave me. Always lurking somewhere is Pain! Can you answer me? All my life I have reasoned with Him, begged Him, and got nothing. Nothing but shattered dreams and a shattered body. What do you have to say about it? Pain, you've been my crutch, my help, my consistent and constant companion.

Why did HE allow those bad things to happen to me? Why was I so ugly? Why did my mother not love me? Why wouldn't my father keep me? Why was I raped? Beaten? Discarded? Scorned, talked about, and ridiculed? Why, and what did I ever do? I was never given a chance. Before I could crawl, others walked out on me. I hadn't made a complete sentence, and people talked against me. I didn't wave a hand, and many fought against me. I was struck down before I got up. I was counted out before I got in. Why?

Before I knew it, I was standing up and asking these questions out loud. I was desperate. I knew that my life was in jeopardy; naturally and spiritually. I knew I could get help right here. Pastor Lee and the other ministers reached for me. Two other ladies, Minister Patricia and Minister Bettye came from their seats and began to pray with me. I could not stop crying. I wept and I cried out for God. Someone started singing. It was the same song the lady was singing back at the church in Red Ash. *Walk with me Lord, while I'm on this tedious journey*. The purple water came. Before I knew it, I had begun to unravel every tangled, sordid, dirty piece of Imogene Marie Jones. I told them everything that I could remember. Nobody stepped back. Nobody turned away. Nobody laughed. Nobody whispered. Nobody pointed fingers. Evangelist Carol, that praying woman, had joined Ministers Patricia and Bettye. They held me up; I couldn't crumble or pass out. I felt strength coming in my body. I heard weeping. This time it wasn't coming from me, it was Sister Denise. She had been the first friend I met when Catherine brought me here. She was always encouraging me. She made it her business to find me whenever I came for a meeting or practice. Not only her, but Sister Evelyn was there also. She would hug me and never let me go home without telling me that she loved me. Sister Evelyn would tell me that if I ever needed to talk, she was there to listen. She was like another Mama. I knew she could tell that I was going through, but she always had a smile and a hug for me. I opened my eyes. Every woman in that room had moved closer to me. Some of them I had never seen. The men in the room encircled the circle of women who were supporting me. It was more than strength. I felt a wave of love infuse me. HE was in the room. I saw HIM. HE was covered in purple. He covered all of us. All at once I knew that HE was the Purple Water!

Immediately a light was shining in front of me. I couldn't see anything or anyone. Was this supposed to be one of those out of body experiences? Had I died and didn't know it? Was I in heaven? No, it was happening again. I was dreaming but I wasn't asleep. I was looking, but my eyes were closed. I was feeling, but I wasn't touching.

I didn't see her at first. I heard someone talking. I know it sounds crazy, but believe me I couldn't make this up. Her voice was light and lyrical. She was speaking, and at the same time it sounded as if she was singing. The light made way and a path led to a giant boulder. Sitting on the boulder was a little girl playing with butterflies. They danced in front of her, sparkling and glowing. Some were orange, and some were red, but most of them were purple. Her face was turned toward something or someone behind her. As the light guided me toward the boulder, her voice became clearer. I could see flowers of all kinds and colors bending in the cool breeze. A big red barn was situated to the right side and it appeared that the butterflies were flying from its open door. I recognized the voice. I mean I had heard it many times before. As she turned to look at me I realized that I was looking at young Imogene Marie Jones. She was grinning and talking a mile a minute. I knew she wasn't talking to me. She kept looking behind her and reaching for the butterflies. Then I saw Him. See may not be the best word to use. If you can see without looking, you know what I mean.

It's that knowing, when you feel something so deeply that you see it before you see it. He touched me. Immediately she stopped reaching for the butterflies when she saw me. Glancing up at Him she silently asked Him if she could touch me too. Waves of purple water washed over me, washed over her, and poured from the door of the barn. The butterflies disappeared. The flowers were gone. The light slowly backed away into the boulder. He gently touched her shoulder and she ran into my arms. I could not remember opening them. I heard her laugh and I can recall her saying, "All is well." I found me when I found Him. I was no longer missing. I was no longer lost.

HE had been there all the time. It was HIM who had saved me, protected me, loved me, and provided for me. He used Big Mama, Lil Bruh, Miss Carolyn, Mr. James, J.C. and Ira. Even Miss Helen had tried to show me. I had no idea. It dawned on me right there and then. I could understand so much more. HE had been speaking to me for a long time. HE didn't make bad things happen to me. HE kept worse things from happening. Pastor Lee explained how sin had caused depravity and wickedness. It was never God's plan to allow these tragedies. But until HE comes to take us back to heaven, we must live in a world which does not know HIM. We have to be HIS hands, hearts, feet, and legs. We have to trust that HE will make everything turn out for our good. God loves us. HE gave His son for us. HE wants us to be with HIM. HE wants us to experience peace, love, and joy. Influences and powers of the devil have come to rob and destroy the earth. But God will never allow us to be utterly destroyed. We have got to trust HIM, and love HIM even when bad things happen. HE will never leave us. HE will never give up on us. HE will turn our mourning into joy, and our ashes into beauty. We must never give up. No matter what! Thank You Jesus! Thank You for Your waters! Your healing waters! Oh, how I love You Jesus! Thank You for loving me!

I don't know how long the Holy Ghost kept us huddled and surrounded by His presence right there. It could have been a minute or an hour. It changed my life forever. I felt like the people in the Upper Room may have felt when they were all together on one accord. I was endued with power. I belonged to something greater than me. I knew that together with the like-minded people, God was going to use me to turn the world upside down. I knew that I had been called and chosen to tell about this Jesus. I felt like the crippled man at the Gate of Beautiful who had been lame from birth, but gained strength immediately when by his faith and the resurrected power of Jesus Christ, he was fully restored. Leaping and jumping for joy; he didn't just go and sit down after being able to walk. He ran to the temple to give God praise. I had to praise Him too! I felt like the woman at the well who had the Living Water and was no longer ashamed of her past. I wanted to tell everybody about a man who knew all about me, and still loved me, still came for me, because it was necessary. I wanted everybody I knew to feel this love and freedom. Today was the first day of the rest of my life.

CHAPTER 9

He reveals mysteries from the darkness and brings the deep darkness into light- Job 12:22

That day when the chains of my past were broken, the bonds of my present were demolished, and the yokes of my future destroyed, was my birthday. I was freed from ropes of negativity and abuse that had intertwined with my existence. So many phenomenal events had occurred. Some of the men from the church had called the police and told them what I had suffered. They were driving me to the police station to file a complaint. Before I got to my home, the police had arrived and arrested Ray. Apparently, he was wanted for some past crimes and in addition to that they had found some drugs on him. This explained some of his behavior toward me. He was not only selling, but using as well. Just as God had used people to show me love, the devil had used people to show me hate. Love triumphs hate though. I didn't have to do a thing. God did it.

Sitting at the feet of Jesus with my head in His lap....as he wiped the tears from my eyes, I heard Him say, "Everything is going to be alright." I trusted Him. I was going to need to hold on and fight the fight of faith like never before. You would think that now, like a good movie, after the hero saved the day, the credits would roll and everyone would live happily ever after. Life is not a movie. We must know that the enemy can not rest or cease until his end in the lake. So, we must stay prayed up and on guard. The best part now is that you really know that you are not alone. Thank God for the Holy Ghost. There will be trials and tests. There will be storms and setbacks. But no matter what, we can never stop trusting and believing that it's going to work out for our good.

I can't get rid of this cold, and I ache all the time. I need to go to Red Ash, talk to Big Mama and Lil Bruh, and get me a drink from the "Anything bottle". I barely rest, working trying to get ahead. I have thrown myself into my designing and working at the church. I found out that Ella and Ray were expecting a child. One of the reasons he didn't push me too much about the sex, is because he was still having sex with her. I dodged that bullet. She also knew that he had a history of hitting women, but she put up with him because he paid her bills.

I decided to go home for the weekend. Big Mama was cooking up everything. She knew that I loved green beans and white potatoes with neck bones. I was counting on some cabbages, yellow rice and cube steak with gravy too. I was going to top it all off with that red velvet cake and sweet tea. I couldn't wait to get back home, if only for a little while.

The first thing I noticed as the bus chugged into Red Ash was the freshly painted boarding house. Big Mama had long since retired and recently it had been turned into a bed and breakfast. Miss Carolyn and Mr. James were no longer "friends", but they were friendly. I was surprised at the excitement I felt as I retrieved my bag from the overhead compartment and made my way to the depot. It had been a while, and maybe I was seeing things differently in more ways than one. But I swear everything looked cleaner and brighter. Even the old wash house looked better. There wasn't any trash swirling around and my old high school looked happy with its renovations.

Big Mama was waving and she looked even smaller than before. Maybe it was me, I had grown up; in more ways than one. She loved me so much. I saw it all over her face. She appeared a little worried about something and I made a mental note to ask her about it later. Lil Bruh had changed the most. In two years, he had lost most of that belly and he was getting around with a little springy step. After hugs and kisses we made our way to the yellow box.

We laughed and talked all the way home. It was like old times; the good part of the old times. Of course, Lil Bruh asked me a riddle. He had to try to stump me. But I knew this one already. He asked a question……

What is greater than God, more evil than the devil, the poor have it, the rich need it, and if you eat it, you'll die?

I told him I knew the answer, it was easy! He called me a smarty pants and tried to tickle me. Okay, Lil Bruh, NOTHING! My answer is NOTHING! The very first line gave me the clue. I knew beyond a shadow of doubt that there was nothing greater than God!

It was good to be home. Thinking about it, I considered it a blessing to be able to come home. Years ago, I heard Big Mama say that the way you leave from a place will determine how you come back in. Always be that one that people are happy when they see you come, and sad when you prepare to leave.

I made my way to my room, unloaded my things and returned to the front porch. It was a beautiful day. Lil Bruh had painted the rocking chairs, and the flower pot was brimming with flowers and plants. Big Mama led me to the side of the house. Escaping from the side porch and climbing towards the sun were some of the most beautiful roses. Big Mama looked at me. I remember planting those roses. I never thought that they would survive, but I was wrong. She led me back to the front of the house, and I found myself counting the steps. She told me that it was time to talk, a long overdue conversation. She said Lil Bruh had gone across the street for Miss Carolyn because they all had something to say. I was curious and excited, with a little trepidation added for good measure.

While we waited for them to return, she stood next to the china cabinet looking at the various pictures and figurines. I watched her take several items out and lovingly replace them. While looking through some papers she came across one with my name on it. She handed it to me. With a puzzled look, I opened the envelope to read what was inside. It was the letter Jacob Kelly had tried to give me 10 years ago.

My Dearest Marie, I would like to share my future dreams with you because I believe you are a part of them. I see just as you see. I won't push you. I know that you have dreams too. Will you meet me so we can talk about it?
I'll wait for you, as long as it takes.

Yours Truly,
Jacob.

P.S. I pray that I will not have to wait long.

Even after all this time my heart was cutting up. I never knew how Jacob felt about me. So much time had passed. I wondered where he was. He must have thought that I wasn't interested since I didn't come to bible study that Wednesday. But if I remember right, that was the time I had taken those pills. I was so distraught. I thought that my life was over before it started. I was mad at everybody. The one time I needed Big Mama the most, I thought that she had let me down. Well, no use crying over spilled milk. I can't imagine what, if any difference our lunch would have made. But it was wonderful knowing that there was someone who really cared about me. He was so young at the time too. I wondered what happened to him. He's probably off and married somewhere with a house full of children.

Miss Carolyn hugged me and didn't want to let me go. She handed me a bag with some cookies and chewing gum in it. I laughed, told her thanks, and proceeded to chew a piece. She said, since Big Mama had cooked all my favorite dishes, she had to bring my favorite treat. Sitting here after quite some time, I'm humbled and blessed to finally feel the love from the people in this room. For so long I was looking for validation and worth when I realized that for my entire life, these people had done all they knew how to do to make sure I felt it. I just didn't see it. I was so busy trying to fit in, trying to prove things, trying to be something that I wasn't. I felt a load lifted.

We were all sitting at the kitchen table. Big Mama, Lil Bruh, and Miss Carolyn had guarded looks on their faces. I shared with them certain key events that prompted my return. I told them about my job, my relationship with God, the lessons I learned from Ray, my successes at work, and my involvement at church. I assured them that I was at peace and I was happy. Little did I know that the next few hours would transform my life even more and solve the world's greatest mystery, according to me! God was not through!

I am finding it quite incredulous still as I am telling you about it. Let me just stick to the facts and offer the details to you. You know me well enough by now that I will get so excited and end up going somewhere else. I am somewhat composed now, but at the time…..well, let me keep going and you'll see what I mean. This is what they told me.

My mother's name was Bella McIntyre. She was Lil Bruh and Big Mama's only daughter. She ran away with James Phillip Jones when she was 15 years old. He was 16. Miss Carolyn is the mother of James Phillip Jones. James was a proud man who loved his beautiful young wife. They were so in love. Considering the countless times, they had been punished and kept apart, it was impossible to stop them from being together. So, when they found them the last time they had run away, it was agreed that as soon as Bella graduated, they could be together. My parents were married in 1947. I was born August 8, 1950. My daddy worked with the railroad in Abbeville, Alabama. My mother was a seamstress. That's where I got my skills from! She could sew anything. She saw it, and she could make it. She made her own patterns and even made curtains, spreads, and covers for chairs.

They lived a few hours away just across the state line. They would visit occasionally. My mother always brought little souvenirs and gifts. That's how a lot of those things in the shed got here. One night while travelling to Marianna, Florida; they stopped to a gas station in Dothan, Alabama. My daddy got into an argument with a group of young white men. They wanted to touch my mother. Apparently, she had exquisite dark skin that looked so soft that they wanted to find out for themselves. The young men followed them as they left the store, hurling insults and throwing bottles. My daddy threw one back and it hit one of the young men. They jumped in their car and tried to force my parents off the road. Trying to escape, my father turned onto a side road that led them into a rural area. They were shot and killed. My daddy was found hanging in a tree next to his burning car. My mother was discovered in a ditch clutching me in her arms. A local farmer heard my cries the next morning as he was preparing his fields for planting.

A few days later, Big Mama, Lil Bruh, and Miss Carolyn had travelled to get me. They decided to take care of me and tell me all of this as I got older. But after all the tragic events that happened in my childhood, it made it impossible for them to explain this back then. My delayed entrance into college was because Big Mama was afraid I would see my birth certificate before they could explain everything. They truly loved me and trusted that the love they had for me would be enough. I couldn't be mad. My sadness was peppered with astounding gratitude. I was thankful to be alive. I was upset that someone had taken precious people from me. I understood so much more now. The voices, the colors, the faces, the smells, and the dreams; it was coming together. But I still had questions.

J.C. and Ira were my uncles. They had grown up vowing to protect me. In the world we lived in, they had to face some harsh realities. But I accepted the unuttered expressions of concern. The ones who killed my parents were never found. People in Alabama knew about it, but no one was willing to inform the authorities because they were white, and my parents were just a couple of uppity black folk from Georgia. They were not. My daddy worked hard for everything. My mommy dressed well because of her gift. It's how ignorance breeds contempt. When people don't know you, they assume. If they are not careful they allow their own shortcomings to create envy and cause them to act in totally unacceptable ways. If we could just get to know people it would erase so much hurt and confusion.

J.C and Ira had spent the better part of their lives trying to find the murderers to no avail. But because of this senseless murder, their careers as undercover agents for the government were launched. It was a rarity for black males to be accepted in this arena. Only a few years before them, James Wormley Jones, a World War I veteran, had become a FBI special agent. My uncles had been policemen in Columbus, Ga. after serving in the army. They had followed many cases but trying to solve my parent's murders was always at the forefront. They vowed to never stop looking until the day they died.

J.C. and Ira had come and taken Lil Bruh away years ago for protection. When he found me in the alley behind Mr. Robert's store, the boy was already dead. Because of the dangerous men Mr. Robert was rumored to be in association with, my uncles thought it best to move Lil Bruh. The murderer had to have seen Lil Bruh in the alley. They may have thought that he saw them too. The murderer has never been apprehended. Mr. Robert had left immediately after his son's funeral.

To say that I was shocked is an understatement. All my life I had convinced myself that Lil Bruh had killed Mr. Robert's son. His hands had bled for days. Now I learned that Lil Bruh had beaten his hands against the doors of the adjacent buildings in anguish, rage, and guilt. He had been unable to protect me, to save me, just as he had failed to be there for my mother. Realizing that they would blame him for Mr. Robert's son, he had run home with me and called J.C. and Ira.

I cried. I cried for my history. I cried for the future I had lost. I cried for family. I cried due to broken promises. I cried because so much time had been given to pain and hate. I cried for mommies and daddies, I cried due to disappointment and missed opportunities. I cried because of misunderstandings. I cried because of secrets. I cried. I've heard that you can't miss something that you never had. That's a lie. It goes up there with the sticks and stones theory. I missed my Mommy. I missed my Daddy.

That wasn't all that I was to learn that day. The two teenagers who tried to rape me had been found right after I left for Atlanta. Apparently, they were visitors at the boarding house for a church conference. They were being sexually abused by one of the preachers in that organization. It had long been known about, but no one did anything to stop it. They ignored it and tried to sweep it under the rug. The big-time preacher was well known, but because he brought in the money and the people, the board allowed it. Some say his wife knew too. But because she liked the fame, the attention, and the applause; this 1st lady wasn't first at all. Why do they call them 1st Lady anyway? Is it because they know they are one in the number? Shoot, I wouldn't ever marry a preacher. The way I have seen them treat preacher's wives is a shame. But that's another story.

The young men had a room across from the wife's room. What a hot mess! The big-time preacher had brought them down here with him. Crooked and perverse is what the bible says. The love of money is evil. Anyway, after one of the services, they had been discovered in bed together by the wife and two of the deaconesses. Rumor has it that the maid had accidentally sent them to the boyfriend's room after someone had requested prayer.

Following this exposure, the young men were determined to show that they were not gay. I was in the right place at the wrong time. They vowed to prove it by "being with" the first woman that they saw. In their drunken stupor and humiliation, they forced me to pay for somebody else's bill. Shortly after this exposure, the church sold the boarding house and many of the congregants left. Big Mama did not tell me about it because they plead guilty and no trial occurred. Since I was just beginning to begin a new journey in my life, Big Mama and Miss Carolyn agreed it was best to let the sleeping dog lie. I don't even know how to take all of this in. I was screaming on the inside! The loudest scream you ever did NOT hear. Was it like the tree in the forest?

You know the one that fell when no one was around? Did it make a sound? Did I scream? Can anyone hear me? Is there any pain? Can you not see it? I can't hold it in any more. That was the old Marie. So, for the next several hours I told them everything that I felt, everything that I had held up and held back. I spoke about the low self esteem I had experienced, every affliction of being different, every cut I sustained from the negative words of others, and every episode of misery. I released every agonizing racking moment of turmoil, regret, and doubt. I realized that they gave me what they could! I KNOW that they loved me. In their attempt to shield me, I had fallen victim to self hate, grief, despondency, and stress.

We all unloaded. It was truly a day of reflection and revelation! Miss Carolyn had brought an old manila envelope with her. She showed me drawings of my parents, her husband, Big Mama, Lil Bruh, and many others. She said my daddy had drawn them. They knew that my talent as an artist had been passed down from him. A small faded picture of a young woman slipped to the floor from among the sketches. She looked like the woman in my dreams. She was one of my imaginary friends.

I had an idea that this would be a good time to just disintegrate into a million pieces! While I was contemplating this, Big Mama took out an old photograph from a drawer under her china cabinet. Silently she handed it to me. Lil Bruh stood closer to me as if he knew that I would crumple. I was looking at my imaginary friend again. This time her hair was loosely plaited and ending below her shoulders. Before the question left my brain, I already knew that she was my mother. She looked so familiar. Lil Bruh confirmed it as I held on to his arm. She was beautiful. I couldn't stop looking at her. Tears dropped on the paper and shocked me back to reality.

I didn't tell them about her being one of my imaginary friends at his time. I just whispered that she looked familiar. Of course, she looks familiar they said. You look just like her! I had never noticed it before. My imaginary friend looked just like me. I guess I did know it deep down inside. But I didn't want to think that I was as crazy as many people thought

I was. It took the actions of talking to yourself to another level. I had to admit the truth though. I was the spitting image of my mother. Except the length of our hair, we could be twins. My mother was beautiful. Even from the old photograph, her skin appeared like liquid. I longed to touch her. I told them that I had believed another lie from the devil and had tricked myself into thinking that I was so ugly that my mommy didn't want me. They all looked at me as if I was demented! What in the world? I said it again and reminded them about finding me on the fish creek by the old bridge. Big Mama and Lil Bruh were speechless.

According to them, Lil Bruh jokingly called me ugly one time when we were playing a game. The story about being found on the fish creek was another one of his stories to justify why I loved fishing so much. He was only playing with me! They couldn't believe that I even recollected the one time that joke was mentioned about the ugly duck. I remembered it all too well. I relived it almost everyday of my life. I thought he was talking about me. Ugly duck playing in the water! Not being ugly was a concept still hard to digest.

Miss Carolyn began to remind me of several incidents where people used to stare at me at school, times when we went to the wash house, Lady Ann's and even at the library. I would never forget those moments. I had memorialized those times. Engraved in the deepest part of my brain, I had no problems remembering. She said people used to talk about how pretty I was when she went to get her hair done. Miss Carolyn said that she never wanted me to act prideful or vain. That's why she used to tell me to always be nice. So, you mean to tell me that for 25 years I have clothed myself in a foul, fictitious cloak of deceit? I was so vulnerable that I allowed a nonchalant comment, a friendly joke, a careless remark, keep me hostage. Words are powerful. Lord help me to be mindful! It was an afternoon of revelations and tears. It's difficult to explain the range of emotions I experienced. Discovering truths and unearthing decades of family history had left me drained. Keeping secrets have a way of depleting your energy. Covering up the results of moral deficiencies and attempting to repair the harmful effects of selfishness adds unnecessary strain and stress. It was a hard job to keep lies a lie. Does telling the truth ever cross a liar's mind?

Chapter 10

Isa 43:2 When thou passest through the waters,
I will be with thee; and through the rivers, they shall not overflow thee: when thou walkest through the fire, thou shalt not be burned; neither shall the flame kindle upon thee.

I have much work to do. Looking at me you would never know how sick I have been. I live my life as if each day is my last. I am thrilled at the way my turnaround has been. I am at peace. Since that dreadful day, when I visited my doctor and received the terrible news that I was positive for HIV, I have not felt so free. I know it doesn't make sense. The destroyer has been destroyed. The thing that was designed to take me out, has been the thing used to bring me up! Come on now! What kind of God is this? I am filled with awe and reverence to my Savior. The many ways that HE has shown HIS love for me is nothing short of a miracle. This is not a death sentence for me. I'm re-writing the chapters of my life. The writing is displayed on the wall like a glaring billboard. I'm a blessed woman!

My list of blessings is growing everyday! I recently received a raise and a new position on my job. I attend church with some awesome men and women. I serve in a ministry in which I get to witness first-hand the power of God in restoring lives. I have a newfound relationship with my grandparents and uncles. I am about to become an "auntie" thanks to Catherine and William. I don't have a man in my life, but I am not lonely. My home has become a place of peace and serenity. I am content and I am experiencing remarkable joy. I know that in times past I was in a state of utter confusion and anguish. I just didn't understand how I could keep being knocked down. But the real story is that I keep on standing because I keep getting back up. I am not going to lie. At first, I thought I would lose my mind. I mean I love the Lord, and I trust Him....but I don't want to die. I have just been born again. I've started on this astounding journey of unearthing my purpose. There are days that I feel like something is still missing. I mean who wants to leave before they live? Why did He allow me to survive the ordeals that would have killed many others? My past involved many obstacles. I was a mess. I was always giving up. I had spent so much time trying to prove things to people, trying to make people accept me, pleasing everyone except Jesus and myself.

That day at the medical center I begged and I pleaded with Him. I bargained and I betted. Then I remembered HIS words to me. *God is our refuge and strength, a very present help in trouble. Therefore, we will not fear though the earth gives way.* You see I had been trying to do it my way, and on my own. Big Mama used to tell me that the Lord won't put no more on you than you can bear. But I found out that was NOT how it actually worked! The truth is, He allows way more than you or I can bear. Burdens, trials, tribulations, death, calamity, sickness, disease, and troubles are heaped upon us. Just like a pile of dirt burying a seed I tell you. I found out that God waits on you and me to call on Him. He knows that we can't handle it. He knows that He can change the very nature, intent, and outcome from the enemy. So, when He said to cast all, roll all our cares on Him, I did. I literally saw Him and a wheel barrow. The old metal kind Lil Bruh used when he was cleaning up around the yard. God was waiting on me to just throw them in, and let Him take care of them! He can make the dirt become our bed and not our grave. Both are places of rest. But it's what happens to us while we're in them that make the difference. I'm living, thriving, and growing in the flower bed of life. That's right, I have decided to live and not die. I'm going to declare the works of the Lord for how ever long I have on this earth! Somehow and some way, God is going to get the glory out of this too!

It's been over a month since my diagnosis; one of the hardest kicks I have had to get up from in my life. Some days are better than others. After I returned from Red Ash Revelation Weekend, I came home with a zeal for life like never before. Big Mama, Lil Bruh, and Miss Carolyn had answered every question

I had and cleared up a lot of things that had entangled me for my entire life. In the midst of the tears, prayers, and disbelief, I was being transformed as every layer of lies was stripped away. My mind was becoming clearer and as a result my vision was too. I've always been able to see, and now that the blood of Jesus has washed my mind, my sight has been enhanced and I am focused as never before. I realize that there is more to me than what I went through. I know that God never left me, even when I felt like He had. Every time and in everything, God was right there. I can't say it enough, I thank Him so much, and there is no way that I would be here without Him.

With a new lease on life, I had made a doctor's appointment to get medicine to get rid of this lingering cold. It wasn't a cold. It wasn't something medicine could clear up. While I was drinking tears and snot on the floor at the doctor's office, I stretched out my hands to Him. It was time to make a decision. I was still trying to figure things out on my own. I had to let it go.

As I was lying on the floor with burning chest pains, praying for a heart attack; He was ridding my heart of contaminated debris with the fire of the Holy Ghost. My afflicted and diseased heart was being ministered to by the Word of the Lord. With every stabbing pain of deception and conspiracy, I felt the Holy Ghost apply a Word to produce healing and strength. No weapon will prosper. I am more than a conqueror. I am not afraid. The Lord is with me wherever I go. The name of the Lord is a strong tower. My heart will not be troubled. I am not afraid. I have the peace of God. I am not afraid. God is my refuge and strength. I will not be shaken because my eyes are always on the Lord. He is keeping me in perfect peace. I am not afraid. The Lord is my refuge and shield. God is preserving my life. I was afflicted to learn of Him. I will call on the Lord in my distress and He hears me. I am not afraid. I recalled bits and pieces of sermons and studies of His word. Instead of waves of tears surging forth, they were replaced by waves of comfort, resilience, and power. The wounded animal departed. Sounds of worship and praise showed up.

I tried to get up. But I felt strongly that I just needed to rest, to just be still. So, I decided to do that. Sometimes we can be too fast for our own good. Trying to get ahead is okay, as long as we're not trying to get ahead of God. Some good intentions and great ideas have been the vehicles for arriving at some unpleasant and painful places. So, I decided to remain where I was, which was in His hands. I had walked through so many doors without paying attention to the sign on the front. Rejection has a job. It is employed as an usher. It holds the door, and opens it to allow fear, un-forgiveness, and bitterness to come in. Then, rejection will introduce you to double-mindedness, shame, and rebellion. It could be years before one discovers why something that happened 5, 10, 20, and even 50 years ago is causing you to FEEL, and ultimately behave in negative ways. Your past affects your present one way or another, good or bad. I'll wait this one out. I'll rest. Sometime later I sat up. Don't ask me how long it was....but eventually, I got up, and I stood up. I can't walk yet. But I'm standing. I can't talk yet. But I'm standing. I can't fight yet. But I'm standing. I had lived so much of my life in a cold dark room, locked from the inside, not knowing that the KEY WAS TUCKED AWAY IN MY POCKET. I allowed the voices of the enemy and other people to become weightier and heavier than the words of the Lord and the loving people he sent to reach me. No longer. I am not a victim. I am victorious. I have concluded that no matter what happens next, I have someone who loves me and would always be there.

I stopped by and checked my mailbox. Since I have been back in Atlanta, Big Mama has been writing me letters with healing scriptures. I read them faithfully. After I told her what the doctor said, she has done nothing but pray and encourage me. What a love, what a faith. There was nothing but a bill from the doctor and a couple of advertisements for furniture. I sat down to look over them and I noticed the message indicator on my answering machine. The message had been left almost two weeks ago. How did I miss that? I guess these little new gadgets take some time learning them. I bet one of them little ones in the junior choir knows how to work it. Playing it back I heard the nurse from the medical center ask me to come in as soon as possible. I made a mental check to call them tomorrow. Opening the letter from them I saw that it was not a bill. The letter stated that they had been trying to reach me for two weeks. There was a medical emergency and I needed to contact them. I made a call to set up an appointment, but the lady told me to just come in. It was urgent! The devil started talking again. It's worse than they thought. You probably need to be in the hospital. You are not going to be able to work. You will lose your job and your home. You will go back home to Red Ash to die a failure. You never made it big. I told you that you would never be anything. I shut Him down quickly:

The LORD is my shepherd; I shall not want. He maketh me to lie down in green pastures: he leadeth me beside the still waters. He restoreth my soul: he leadeth me in the paths of righteousness for his name's sake. Yea, though I walk through the valley of the shadow of death, I will fear no evil: for thou art with me; thy rod and thy staff they comfort me. Thou preparest a table before me in the presence of mine enemies: thou anointest my head with oil; my cup runneth over. Surely goodness and mercy shall follow me all the days of my life: and I will dwell in the house of the LORD for ever. Psalm 23

Sidebar: One definition of fear by Merriam-Webster is; an unpleasant often strong emotion caused by anticipation or awareness of danger. Fear is the friend of rejection. Fear uses the lack of knowledge and the unknown to fuel its assault on your beliefs. Who do you believe God is? Do you believe what God said about you? Why believe the devil then? What you don't know can paralyze or slow you down. When you don't know the truth, the enemy plays the dangerous game of WHAT IFS, and your perception is colored by the state of your mind. If you don't fight the good fight of faith, then fear will strangle the life out of you.

Okay, that was two of my cents. I'm headed to the medical center. I'm prayed up, and I am trusting God. The calmness that I'm wearing is a part of my new attire. I will get used to this. My confidence in God has never been at this level. I'm a witness that what the enemy meant for my bad, God allowed it for my good. The nurse called me to the back, and the information I received was enough to make me run around the building.

Apparently, a terrible mistake had been made. My lab results had been improperly handled. At least that's the only explanation the staff could offer. They were still learning things about HIV and AIDS. The first recorded case had been only 20 years prior in the late 1950s. I DID NOT have HIV. They did tell me to come back in a few months to be retested, but at this time all my tests were negative. I didn't know whether to run, shout, fall out, or cry. I never imagined a rejoicing like this. I praised God all by myself. I don't know how long I celebrated Jesus in that doctor's office! In the same office where the enemy tried to hand me a death warrant, God was giving me a certificate of life! Hallelujah! I knew that my life would never be the same. I opened the windows of my heart and declared the greatness of the Lord! HE did it! Hallelujah! I passed the test. The devil lied. I believed the report of the Lord! HIS hands have been on my life every since I been here. I have His knowledge, His truth residing in me. I know that I know that I know! I know my purpose. I know that I must help other people. I know that I am worthy. I know that I can make a difference. I know that I have value. God wants me. HE WANTS ME! Glory! Every evil thing, every negative word, every cut, every tear, every kick, every look, every whisper, every slip, every fall, has been covered by the blood of Jesus! Hallelujah! He did it for me, and I must tell it everywhere that I go! HE will and can do the same thing for you! One day I'll find Sarah Delois Benson. One day I'll drink me a ginger ale. One day I'll stop hating green frogs. One day. But today I'm taking one step at a time. One day at a time. Because I know I'll make it.

CHAPTER 11

A NEW BEGINNING

I couldn't wait to get to bible study tonight. As I left the bathroom, Minister Patricia was coming down the corridor from the pastor's study. She said that we were going to have a special guest speaker tonight. I just wanted to hear the word. I came expecting, and the Lord was going to bless me some more. During prayer service, I made my way to the altar. I want you to know something, that song is so true. Look at your hands they look new, look at your feet and they do too. Thank You Lord. I looked and felt brand new.

Pastor Lee and some other ministers came to the pulpit. I wasn't paying any attention to the guest. I was so excited, because all day I had been in worship mode. After finally getting off the phone sharing my praise report with Big Mama, Lil Bruh, Miss Carolyn, Catherine, and Pastor Lee; I had a vision that I couldn't understand.

I was in a grassy field with beautiful flowers. The grass was so green and almost to my knees. I wanted to run freely and I noticed a path in the center of the field. The cleared path opened to a river with the most beautiful water I had ever seen. The water was so clear and as I walked towards it, I could see a lot of fish swimming. Beyond the far bank of the river I saw a man dressed in purple and gold. I couldn't see his face, but he was calling my name. But he was calling Imogene. I never used that name. It had been years. He was asking me to come and help him gather the fish. Then the picture went away.

We were about to start. I found my regular seat and began searching for my pen. I heard the voice instruct us to turn to Luke 15, starting at verse 4. I thought I was back in Red Ash experiencing my imaginary friends in the old shed. The voice sounded so familiar. He continued with his opening statements.

He said I want to begin by talking about the lost and found. While you are finding the scripture; let me begin by talking to you about loss. When you lose something or someone precious to you, you can become distraught and stressed. He said however, no matter how long it takes, you keep looking. Pray and do what you need to do to find them. Make sure that when you find what has been lost, you never let it go. Our speaker was Jacob Kelly. He was looking right at me.

The next few weeks went by so fast, and I hardly had time to catch my breath. Before I knew it, I was holding on to Mr. Charlie McIntyre's arm as he escorted me down the aisle. Who would have thought that I would be in this place? I had never imagined such joy and excitement. It was more than a new beginning. What I was trying to contain in my belly, in my mind, and in my heart, was impossible. I could almost trace the invisible cords of love, joy, and peace that securely held me.....The intangible laces of serenity and contentment wrapped me ever so lovingly next to God in a way that words could never describe.

Every step I made to the altar fastened my future to Jacob's. I could see it....the ends of my cords attached with his. Becoming one; magical and mystical, while being divine and purposed. This is how it's supposed to be. This is how God intended it and planned from the very beginning. There were some delays and detours, but God always had a plan. A lie doesn't care who tells it. What matters is what you believe and what counts is who you listen to. I have come a long way, and I still have some ways to go. But I'll get there. I have everything that I need to make it. I want to receive everything that God has for me, and at the same time I want to give Him everything that I have for Him. It's not enough for me to "get it". My dream is for everyone to "get it". As Lil Bruh and I get closer to Jacob I realize what a cherished love looks like. I'm so grateful that I didn't die. I'm thankful for another day to be me. I owe God everything! I know that every second is a new beginning, and that also means that there has to be some endings. I end associations and fellowships with everything and everybody that is not in God's plan for me. I end every negative agreement I made knowingly or unknowingly. I cancel every vow, every plot, and every interference, in my life; and the lives of those connected to me. In Jesus' name, amen!

I'm not going to play with you. Let me be clear. This hasn't been easy at all, and I almost didn't make it....so many times I gave up, I messed up, and I failed. But the best evidence that God is real is that I'm still standing here today. As I glance at the people who have come today to help me celebrate another promise from the Lord, I am reminded again that the devil is a liar. Big Mama's smile lit up the church. The love from her enormous heart is blinding. All those years, I mistakenly thought that the yellow box glowed from the sun, instead of the Son. The Son inside of her. I treasure her and her devotion tremendously. Her dedication to the Lord was always an indication of His greatness, whether I accepted it, paid it attention or not. That's just how He is. He's there all the time, keeping us even when we don't want to be kept. Thank You Holy Ghost! Miss Carolyn and Mr. James stood together with loving looks of approval, nodding as I floated past their pew. Ira and J.C. were not smiling, but their eyes were laughing. It's something about those eyes. What a difference time makes! My "babies", the ones that the Lord has trusted me to mentor were gathered side by side, another testament to the power of God and His truth. I'm looking forward to the opportunities to share God's restoring and redeeming grace with them. My church family unselfishly proved that love is an action word. They were still lifting me up as usual; the beautiful hands and feet of God endearing me to them even more. They were responsible for the enveloping sense of gaiety and festivity. Everything was breathtakingly lovely. The sanctuary had been transformed into a winter wonderland.

When I joined my hands with Jacob, the most beautiful purple and orange butterfly hovered in front of us. As the thought left my mind, "Does anyone else see this?" Jacob squeezed my hand, pulled me closer to his side, and whispered in my ear,

"Yes. I see!" I'm blessed in so many ways. It's not so much in what I have; it's so much more in what I don't have. I don't have guilt or shame. I left bitterness, regret, and un-forgiveness some time ago. Doubt and condemnation no longer know my name or address. I'm not friends with fear. I stopped hanging out with negativity. I have nothing to do with ugly. Yes, I'm blessed. God said it, and I believe it! I am beautiful. I am smart. I am valued. I am loved. I am important. I am needed. I am chosen. I am strong. I am special. I matter. I'll never agree with what the devil says about me. He's such a liar.

Yes, such a liar. He lied about a lot of things. As I write these lines to share my story with you I'm having to balance my time with helping Jacob in our ministry, designing a new clothing line, and taking care of our identical twins Joseph and Joshua. Yes, that's right, you read right. After all the agonizing and traumatic events throughout my life, God has remained ever faithful. I am a mother! God did it!

Jacob and I are humble servants of House of Faith Outreach Ministry. My husband has been working for the Lord since graduating from theology school. Upon graduation, Jacob returned to assist his father in Red Ash. He visited Big Mama to inquire about me, and she told him that I was engaged to be married. After about six months, he left for Africa to start a church, build schools and hospitals. He said the short time mission trip turned into several years. It was an opportunity to serve others that led him into a friendship with Pastor Lee. A particular ministry organization had missions all over the world. They decided to do a work in the United States. They reached out to Jacob after observing his dedication and success abroad. Jacob was one of the evangelists chosen to lead a group and build a community-based outreach center in a disadvantaged neighborhood in Atlanta. After meeting with some of the leaders and finding them to be more concerned with wealth and fame, Jacob expressed his thoughts and dismissed himself. As he was leaving the building, Pastor Lee left also and they struck up a conversation. It turns out they became great friends and kept in touch for years. They invested their own money to start a nonprofit organization to mentor young men and women. Several of these young people have given their lives to Jesus. My husband served primarily in Africa. He and Pastor Lee had developed a personal and professional relationship over the years. Jacob was building people and families in Africa while my Pastor was doing the same here. Unlike Pastor Lee, Jacob had remained single devoting himself completely in his ministry. However, he said he had a dream that his wife was waiting for him back here.

Three months before Jacob taught bible study, he had met with Pastor Lee. They were in the office when my husband was looking at pictures from our Community Fun Day. He was shocked to discover that I was right here serving the Lord with his long-time friend, single and free! He shared his feelings with Pastor Lee and was determined that He would not lose me again. He said the Lord told him it was not time yet to approach me, so he waited. Rightly so, God was still doing a new thing in me. I wasn't ready at that time to reconnect with Jacob. Thank God for a man who heard and obeyed the Holy Spirit! My pastor questioned him endlessly. Was he sure? A long time had passed. He knew immediately from the pictures that it was me. Pastor Lee was talking about how incredible our story was, like something from a book or a movie. The big scrapbook had many pictures of our ministry events. But the one that caught Jacob's attention was one of me handing a box of food and supplies to some neighborhood friends. He said the dream that he had in Africa made sense. In it, he could only see the back of me. The woman in his dreams was standing in a house packing up food and toiletries. He could see her loading them on the back of a truck. So, the scrapbook just happened to be opened to that page when he visited this particular time.

I couldn't believe that he had known since the night of my high school graduation that he was going to marry me. The Lord truly does work in mysterious ways! Now together we are one, introducing Jesus Christ to the world, beginning right here at home in Red Ash. If you can't help the people in your neighborhood, how can you help those in other nations?

I am so appreciative of the supernatural power of God. I mean how else can I do what I do? Big Mama and Miss Carolyn help me with our babies. The babies that I was never supposed to be able to have. He gave me a double blessing. Identical little boys who remind me of God's grace and mercy every single day! Can you imagine our shock when we learned that I was expecting? We were in Africa and Jacob thought I was ill because of the various foods that I wasn't used to eating. Well, within a few weeks we found out how 9 months of bad eating habits were turning out. Now, two years later, and defying the odds, are two little miniatures of my Daddy. Granny Carolyn says it's like God reversed time whenever she looks at them. She is quick to let me know that the tears I see sometimes are those of joy. God is working on all of us. Joshua and Joseph's birth drew Granny Carolyn to have a real relationship with The Lord! Ain't God good. Due to my past medical history and increased age, Joseph and Joshua were the furthest thoughts away. But God! He had a plan. He always has. It's not over until God says it's over.

Now I'm not sitting here pretending like it's all been a breeze. Problems come and try to visit at times, but we welcome them to leave before they can come through the door. My husband and I are a team. We make sure to keep each other priority, after God of course. We have had some incredible times with the Lord. One day I might have to tell you about some of them.

Anyway, I am a living witness that God is a friend, a healer, a provider, and a faithful advocate. He has done so many great things for us. Jacob loves me unconditionally. He is a hard worker, and yet he makes time to show me how much he cherishes who I am. Our marriage is a testament to the sovereignty of a wise God. During our visit to South Africa for our honeymoon, my husband had an opportunity to preach in Southern Namibia. The vision I had of the man asking me to help him with the fish was brought back to my memory. Jacob's purple and gold dashiki flowing in the wind was so surreal. At the close of his altar prayer, he invited me to stand with him and continue the Lord's work. If I could just explain the joy! Let me tell you, I'm a witness to the faithfulness of a loving God! To anyone who has ever been told that they don't matter, or that they won't make it, and will never have anything, don't believe it. You are not what they say! You never answer to the enemy's voice. Trust God no matter what it looks like or feels like. I've come a long way and I know that with God on my side I win every time. He will not let my enemies triumph over me! Not ever!

He will do the same for you too. God is not like us. He doesn't look at our clothes, jewelry, money, or cars. He considers the inside. Our hearts and minds are what He desires to make whole. So, you fell. Okay, it's harder than it's ever been. I get that you are tired.....but hold on...help is on the way! Actually, it's already here! Don't quit. Don't give up. Don't turn back. Stay with God! There is NOTHING too hard for Him! He won't let you down. NEVER!

When we returned to the United States the blessings of the Lord ran us down and took over our lives. My gifts from the Lord; a loving husband who lives for the Lord, beautiful healthy children, a thriving ministry and a growing business, supportive family, and genuine friendships. I asked the Lord, "What more could I ask for?"

Chapter 12

And we know that all things work together for good to them that love God, to them who are the called according to His purpose. Rom 8:28

I was sitting on Big Mama's porch enjoying the sunshine. Everyone was inside feasting on the last of Big Mama's red velvet cake. The rhythmic cadence of the rocking chair was lulling me to sleep. The red paint was peeling from the side of the barn. The timber had weathered many storms. However, the walls were still standing. I saw butterflies flying into the owl hole. My mother stood at the entrance of the door holding grains of wheat. I followed her inside as she stepped over a wide board covering the threshold. Inside on the barn floor were piles of husks and straw. She pointed to a large table with a coarse piece of white cloth protecting it. Seeds were piled on the table and some other people were gathering them into containers. She kept pointing to the name written on the side of the containers. I read it. She was telling me something important.

When I told Jacob about the dream he suggested that we pray and ask God for direction. He felt as I did; that it meant more than an emotional occurrence during sleep. Jacob said when he walked towards me on the porch my eyes were blinking rapidly, I was breathing deeply as if I couldn't catch my breath, and I was chanting the same word over and over. Because my husband truly knows me, in every sense of the word, with his understanding of spiritual matters, he was certain that I had been given some useful information. I don't have the time to explain how God has worked within me to bring comfort, peace, and joy to others in this way, but it was for me at this time! I know the Holy Spirit is powerful! He's real and He can do what He wants to, how He wants to, and when He wants to! Hallelujah! This dream was so real. You know what I mean? You just can't explain it but you know that "something was trying to tell you something", but He is not a something, He is God.

We called my uncles and they listened to what I had to say. They didn't hesitate. One thing about this journey I have been on, God has shown himself to me as well as the people around me. They asked us to meet with them at Uncle Ira's home in Columbus, Ga. He said if we were going to go any further then we would already be close to Alabama. Even though they both had retired from the government, they had made their homes in Muscogee County. Citing his ties with Fort Benning and ex-military friends; Uncle J.C chose to move there and has done very well establishing a security company for various textile businesses. Uncle Ira and his wife own an art gallery and museum. It seems that Uncle Ira had a gift of painting also. Inspired by Alma Woodsey Thomas, he explored other artistic interests which prompted him to also teach art at the local youth center.

I didn't tell my uncles all the details over the phone. When Jacob and I arrived at our hotel, Uncle Ira was waiting in the lobby. After greetings and hugs, we checked in and went to meet Uncle J.C. at the restaurant. My grandparents, all three of them had practically begged Jacob and me to allow them to watch the twins for a few days. It was going to take all three of them too! So, Jacob and I drove to Columbus, GA for a few days. Emerging from the restaurant with the beloved men of my family, I was determined even more to move forward with the bits of information my dream had provided. It seems that the name on the containers I had seen in the dream, PARRETT, had also been the name of one of the suspects for the murder of my parents. It could never be proven. They were concerned that now almost 30 years later, too much time had passed. J.C. and Ira took my information and promised to make some phone calls. They would contact us as soon as possible.

Before we would return to Red Ash, Jacob and I decided to have some us time. Here I was married to a preacher. The very thing I didn't want turned out to be the best thing that God prepared for me. Be careful saying what you won't do, and what you don't want.

My husband made the difference in this ordeal. He covered me; mind, body and soul. We visited some of the city's museums and parks. It was interesting touring the home of the inventor of Coca Cola, and enjoying the history of the industrial development, the tragic wars, and the ongoing revitalization of the downtown area.

I awoke to bells ringing. It was the phone on the bedside table. Uncle J.C. told us to hurry and get dressed. We were taking a drive to Dothan, Alabama. I was showering and the tears came out of no where. I heard the bathroom door open and Jacob stepped into the bathtub with me. My heart was pounding and old thoughts tried to invade my mind again. Just as the water was flooding over my body, the outdated memories were flooding my mind. Jacob held me. He covered me with prayer as he covered me with his body. He encouraged me to let it all out. He reassured me that God was still with me, and He was still in control. I needed to hear his soothing words. Jacob asked me to let God hold the weights. He knew that even though I had trusted God, and loved Him, I was still reluctant to let go of something. As Jacob held me and prayed, I recognized the load. It was CONTROL. I had never fully relinquished control. I thought that I had totally surrendered, but my husband knew that I had not. So, I know that I wasn't fooling God either. Jacob said I did not have to be strong all the time. He understood that even the strongest person needs help sometimes. He promised me without saying a word that I could count on him. As my husband lifted me from the bathtub, God was showing me that He was lifting from my struggles. Another reason to fall in love all over again with the both of them! After a little delay, we got dressed and met the others.

Uncle Ira was driving and humming. The mood was positive. Their contacts, current investigators, were meeting with us to discuss some new information. I was excited, and I was thinking about my parent's road trip about 28 years ago. A lot had changed of course. Peanuts, not pine was being successfully produced. Along with Sony, the nuclear plant is one of the largest employers in the region. My daddy had worked the railroad in the late 1940s. It was honest and hard work. From all the stories I've heard about him from my grandparents, he was what one would call a visionary. He was very ambitious, and he wanted the best for my mother and me. After I was born my parents had decided to move to Florida since my daddy had been given a job with the logging railroad. They were on their way to look for a house when they were murdered. One thing that had not changed as much was the overall law enforcement viewpoints toward minorities. This was the 70's, but everybody was not giving free love and experiencing black power.

We pulled into the parking lot of an old peanut mill. The huge clock embedded in the concrete wall must have been broken. I checked my watch commenting about how time seemed to be going slow. I guess I was just anxious. Jacob reminded me of the time zone difference. Here in Dothan, they were an hour behind us. The drive had taken less than an hour and 45 minutes.

We made our way inside, and two men were seated at a table. They greeted J.C. and Ira like old friends. After some brief introductions, we all sat down and again God showed up. He's just like that. He's always looking out for us and making ways out of no way. Just when I thought I would never know the full story surrounding my parent's murder, I was given folders of pictures and notes. They had removed the pictures of their bodies, but I could see and feel the cold evil as my eyes swept across the pages. The detectives had a box with some clothing in it, but I was more interested in the information about Parrett and his friends. The notes described the location and placement of the bodies, but not much else. I was disappointed. But as I turned the last page I read about the scene at the barn. No one had ever known anything about a barn. Evidently, this information was not even given to Big Mama either. So, when I described it to my uncles, they knew that there was something to it. According to the report, before killing my father, three men raped my mother inside of the barn. They don't know whether he witnessed it or not. Such sorrow came over me. To know the horrific ending of my parent's last days on earth was almost too much. But Jacob was there, and the Holy Ghost was too. I stared at the handwriting.

I heard her screaming....The familiar sense of fear and dread blanketed me as my mother clutched me to her breast. I smelled the sweat and blood from her neck. I heard her begging and pleading with them not to hurt me. I saw them dragging her disfigured and mutilated body outside to an open area. She was still breathing and her efforts to hold onto me were becoming harder. I felt her fingers grope for me since her eyes were swollen shut. I heard them laughing as they spit on us. Two hands pulled me from her clutches. Unable to speak, I heard her moaning. I was not strong enough. I don't want to see anymore. Remove the taste and smell of death please! Stop it please. I certainly need You now Lord!

I had to go to further. My uncles thought that it would be too much, but Jacob knew that I was too close to breakthroughs. I had to experience this. I had to be able to comprehend the healing power of Jesus completely. I was already aware in a very real manner, the awesomeness of God, and this would further seal the confidence I would need to complete my work for Him.

There were three names on the report. Two of the men had died not long after my parent's murder; horrible train accidents. The remaining suspect, Jimmie Parrett lived about 30 miles away in Enterprise, Alabama. He had been interviewed years ago, but they did not have enough evidence then to bring charges. They still didn't. All they had was a grieving young woman's unexplainable possession of facts. It was only because my uncles had been held in such high esteem from certain officers that we even had this opportunity.

These officers could tell that with or without them, I was headed to Enterprise. While my uncles talked to the higher ups that they knew, Jacob and I talked to our High Up. After forever had passed, we were on our way. Taking a few wrong turns, and consulting the map several times, we pulled up to a big white house. I was told to stay in the car. The detectives, along with my uncles walked towards a dilapidated Victorian home. The paint was faded, and the roof was caving in on one side. The large porch had boxes of clothes, books, and household items stacked to the windows. It looked as if someone was clearing out an abandoned house. They knocked and went around the back. There was nothing to identify if it was still inhabited or whose residence it was. No mailbox on the porch or in the yard. This was normal since most of those in rural areas picked their mail up at the local post office. I sat upright as an uneasy feeling overcame me. An extreme bout of nausea overwhelmed me. I needed fresh air.

They were headed back, and I jumped out of the car to meet them. Curtains from a second story window moved. I pointed and the officers asked me to get back in the car. Slowly the front door opened, and a frail looking white man stood in the doorway. Before the officers could greet him, the man turned towards me and said, "I knew you were coming back to get me. I'm sorry what I did to you. Now I'm ready to go."

I was speechless as I watched him put a gun in his mouth. I closed my eyes as I heard the gun explode. Jacob carried me to Uncle Ira's car. I sat in the back seat the entire time the necessary procedures were carried out. Many people came and left. I didn't notice any of them. I didn't feel remorse or happiness. I felt slighted, but I knew that God was going to work this out in me too. They found all the evidence they needed. Parrett had kept a writing tablet with the confession by his bedside. He was dying of cancer, and he wanted it to be found at his death. The gun he committed suicide with is the same one used to shoot my father. They did not use it on my mother, she bled to death. The confession stated that they tied my daddy up and beat him. They shot him in his legs to keep him immobilized.

After beating him, they were intent on making him watch as they each were going to take turns raping my mother. His heart could not take it and he had a heart attack before they even touched my mother. I gained some solace that he did not die with those images in his mind. Still, it did not diminish the fact that these men had taken away people who I had grown to love in life and greater in death. Parrett went on to pen that the other two men burned my daddy's car because they didn't think a colored man should be able to drive a vehicle like that.

He continued to confess that the other two men had wanted to drown me, but he was unable to go through with it. The letter stated that they had taken me to the Choctawhatchee River to get rid of me. As he submerged me in the water, he wrote that a force in the water pushed him back. He said he tried to push me under several times, but he would be pushed back. He said he felt hands on his wrists preventing him from just releasing me in the water. After the 5th attempt, he was too fearful to try again. Unable to leave me in the river, they left and he was too fearful to try again. They left me at a church with my mother's sweater wrapped around me.

It was a lie that a farmer had found me in a ditch in my dead mother's arms. Parrett and his friends had made up the lie so it could circulate and throw off the investigation. You know how rapidly lies and rumors spread in small towns. It only takes one person. Before you know it, "they say" will have you dead and buried when you're up walking and breathing. "They say" will swear they saw it all and will describe every lie in detail. "They say" will have you believing a lie and disputing the truth. "They say" has caused more hurt and harm than all wars and calamities combined.

There were other details about the two men and their deep hatred for black people in his confession. I didn't need to read any more to know that. It was only evil and hatred that could drive a human to do inhuman acts, such as they did. It was a sign of the times. Being hated and despised because of the color of your skin.

I was ready to go back to Red Ash after one more stop. Jacob knew me so well. Before leaving this area, he asked the investigators for the location of the actual crime scene.

Uncle Ira drove down an old country dirt road. The ruts were cut deep. Symbolic of my pain at the time. He had to drive slowly because the tires were vibrating and the entire car was shaking violently if he picked up speed. I knew that where we were headed was necessary for the health of my mind. I didn't want to wonder and wander later on. Jacob held my left hand and with his right hand he rubbed my shoulder.

I saw the red barn from a distance. It stood bright red against a backdrop of white, purple, and red flowers. It didn't look like the barn in my dream because this barn was freshly painted and glistened in the sunlight. As we drew nearer, I felt an overwhelming sense of peace. Uncle Ira's jaw was clinched tightly, and Uncle J.C. was wiping tears from his eyes.

Her bright golden yellow cotton dress contrasted sharply with her chocolate face. As she smiled, the sun's rays meekly withdrew so as not to compete with the brightness of it. Golden flecks landed on my face and arms as I lifted my face and stretched my arms to the sky. As she turned to walk behind the barn, the man with Joshua and Joseph's face hugged her and waved at me. Together at last!

We stood outside for a few more minutes, and I knew it was time to go. I tugged on their arms and we made our way back to the car. I remember years ago telling Lil Bruh that I was going to find this barn one day. I had no idea in my childish ramblings that I was speaking into existence this very thing. I had no idea how my words or declarations would become powerful tools against the enemy of God's Kingdom. That's another story.

Final Sidebar: Everything you need, you already have. It's in you. Remember that the plans of God always outweigh what anyone thinks. It's not just a cliché. With God all things ARE possible. You have to decide and make up your mind to believe what God has already said. Plan according to His purpose. Set goals. Write it down. Make it plain. Don't wait on things to happen. Don't wait on people to get with you. Pray, seek God, and then obey. Act on what you believe. When you work on God's plan, prepare for His purpose, and trust the process, you can never lose. No matter how you feel, what anyone else will say, where you have been, or what you have done.....God is real. He will make it all work together. He said that He loves you. He said that He would never leave you. He said He would never withhold any good thing from you. He said that you were victorious. You can trust Him. He has NEVER lied.

Well, I'm back to taking care of my Father's business. I'm doing well and I'm getting more excited as I prepare for our weekly Women's Therapy 101 at House of Faith. God has sent women from every walk of life to this service. We meet to encourage one another, build up faith, share testimonies, teach the word of God, sing, cry, eat, and pray. I was giving back to these women the way Minister Patricia, Elder Bettye, Evangelist Carol and many others had done for me. Pastor Lee had told me that this day was coming. To someone who had so little, and had lost so much, I couldn't have ever imagined that I would be standing in front of people testifying and praising the Lord, and teaching His word! But here I am. God did this! This ministry God ordained me to start for women had allowed me to see miracles, signs and wonders of salvation, healing and deliverance often. I was excited for our future and thankful for a family that pushed and supported me.

Almost every seat was filled tonight for WT-101. We were just about to start the bible study when the door opened and a woman walked in appearing nervous. The honey from the "Anything Bottle", said, "Hello, my name is Delois Benson, and I was told that I could find help here." Looking up to the heavens, and silently thanking the Lord, I reached for her hand as I responded, "Hello, I'm Imogene Kelly; you may remember me as Marie Jones..

Falling Up

by Mistry Troutman

Backwards.....crumbling......the wave of hate sent me reeling...Words spilling from your lips, too heavy to remain in your mouth, penetrating my heart, and taking every love letter back....You are pain....you are shame.....you are heavy....I am kneeling! Forward...I'm moving...looking up, I SEE the sound of laughter slippery slivers of promise, gently turning and washing my soul, covering my wounds, lifting me up, I'm standing..... I am healed.....I am well.....I am free.....thank you Lord for after!

Epilogue

I grabbed the broom and spit on it after she swept my foot with it. I believe she did it on purpose. I know she don't like me. She would love to see me riding in the back seat of THAT car. She has never wanted me here. Here is anywhere next to her. She blames me for everything evil, everything bad, and everything painful. Since the day she birthed me I have been the main ingredient for her recipe of regret. My mother hates me.

I told her what he did. That's why she hates me. She didn't believe me. So, I stopped telling her. Now it's my fault? Since them folk come over here she upset. She won't talk to me. She won't even cuss me out. She upset because of her stamps. If they cut her stamps off she gone be real mad. I was only answering the teacher question. She asked me why I be so sleepy. I told her because I do not sleep at night. I have to fight him off. He doesn't care if I am asleep or not. The last time I woke up to him inside me of me he just covered my mouth and kept jumping on me. I should be hating her. Jesus help!

Now where that come from? Jesus? What He got to do with this? He doesn't fool with me, and I don't fool with Him. It didn't mean a thing, a slip of the tongue. Just something I said. Didn't mean nothing. Delois, you need to watch what you say girl…….